MARC

MARC

A SENTIENT PERMANENT MARKER ROMANCE

IMOGEN KNOWED

Papeback ISBN: 978-1-972670-03-3
Ebook ISBN: 978-1-972670-28-6

To all the high-masking, high-anxiety neurodivergents who feel they have to perform to be loved.

CONTENT WARNINGS

This book has explicit descriptions of sexual acts.

While all sex is consensual, some acts may be considered dubious or coerced.

A main character expresses suicidal ideation.

CHAPTER 1
ALICE

If someone had told me last month I'd be lying on my back with a Sharpie in my cunt, clutching the edge of my comforter like a lifeline and waiting for a magic show, I probably wouldn't have believed them. *Probably. I definitely would have asked a few follow-up questions.*

But here I am!

I'm sprawled across my mattress, naked from the waist down, knees tipped outward, holding a desiccating Sharpie more than 4.2 inches inside my pussy: 4.44 inches, actually, as verified by Gage.

Gage's face is a hopeful moon orbiting my pelvis, lit by nerves, awe, and the slow-building thrill of someone about to witness the miracle of his girlfriend's minge materializing a man from a marker. He asked me to turn this marker into a human before it ran out of ink, and I am nothing if not a very accommodating, very stupid girlfriend.

Gage vibrates at the bedside like an expectant father, but it's not the birth of his firstborn he's expecting: he's anticipating his best friend's emergence from the sticky cave of my vagina. Although, to quote him, "friend isn't entirely accurate," as the two have never met—since one of them doesn't exactly exhibit any form of consciousness…yet.

I try not to think too hard about Gage's past "relationships," because the existential minutia of the whole thing makes my head spin and, if I'm being honest, "don't think too hard about it" has always kinda been my life's motto.

Unfortunately, that philosophy is about to get stress-tested. Because if this works—*and past precedent and my mother both say it will*—this marker is eventually going to stop being a marker and start being a person.

And that's where the dread creeps in…because the last time I did this, I didn't think nearly hard enough. Gage is living proof of that.

To be clear, Gage is amazing. Gage is wonderful. Gage is enthusiastic and sweet and has the emotional transparency of a man not raised in the patriarchy.

Right now, he's beaming in that way only someone with absolutely zero life experience can beam. His eyes—ridiculously hyper-cerulean—are wide with awe, and he's smiling so big it looks like he might unhinge his jaw and swallow the entire moment whole.

He's an adorable, earnest dork, and I truly love him. But Gage is also the physical manifestation of a request I didn't fully think through.

A little over a month ago, he was a plastic ruler. Now he's a flesh-and-blood, hyper-literal himbo with anxiety issues and a strong desire to measure everything. My boyfriend. My number one fan. A man who looks at me like I'm a goddess, the creator of the universe—which, I guess, for him I kinda am. I created him, but I'm not a goddess—just blessed (*cursed?*) by a god. You'd think faux goddess status would involve more silk sheets and grapes dangling in front of me and fewer office supplies in my puss, but you work with what you get.

To say I don't learn from my mistakes would be the understatement of the century. But saying that out loud starts sounding dangerously close to admitting Gage might have been a mistake, and I'm not quite emotionally prepared to consider that as more than a fleeting thought experiment. So, I continue lying here in this act of weird, reckless faith.

This curse will happily give me exactly what I ask for—and none of what I actually need—so I should probably aim a little higher than "dorky, golden retriever with abs and a twelve-inch cock."

I close my eyes and try to envision the perfect man—or maybe woman. I haven't decided which I'd prefer.

Someone capable.

Someone stable.

Someone who might, theoretically, take care of me for once.

But every time anyone remotely clear begins to solidify in my mind, Gage does something distracting, like right now—

My eyes fly open at the squeak of flesh on mylar to find Gage fidgeting. And for him, fidgeting usually amounts to measuring. He's measuring a "Welcome!" balloon with a bright blue tailor's tape, which I have come to learn he can materialize from thin air whenever he wants. He just opens his hand, and some measuring device appears. Even though he doesn't seem to need it; he can eyeball a length to the nearest tenth of a centimeter.

He sees me watching him and, with the embarrassment that would make you think I caught him playing with his cock, releases the balloon and returns the measuring tape to the realm from which it came.

The balloon bounces back to the ceiling, making me tense as I prepare for it to pop. It doesn't, it just bounces languidly against the ceiling. But my racing heart doesn't slow, and this marker hits a spot within me that makes me think: *Fuck, I shouldn't be doing this.*

I'm kind of going through a lot right now.

Maybe bringing another life into this world is not the best thing for me.

I should probably, like, actually work through my feelings around all the life-altering revelations I've been avoiding reflecting too intensely on…

First, I learned I can turn objects into people by shoving them inside my cooch. Then I learned I'm half calculator watch since my dad used to be one. In fact, this magical vaginal ability has been in my family so long that if I were to do a DNA test, I bet it would say, "99.9999999999% former-object that used to be phallic enough to be shoved into a vagina." Then, I had to teach Gage to be a human, not a ruler. And, I think I've just been avoiding thinking about all of it by fucking him—a lot.

The fact that Dionysus, the Greek god of essentially avoiding your sads by drinking wine, partying, and fucking, gave this gift—blessing, curse, whatever—to my family is not lost on me.

Too late to turn back now, I guess, because this thing is already inside me, gathering whatever magic my transmutation twat has to offer.

Gage returns his attention to adjusting the Funfetti cupcakes he baked for the occasion, and I try to return my attention to the supposed miracle I'm trying to manifest out of this knock-off marker.

It's not even a real Sharpie. It's just a generic marker that's clearly trying to ride Sharpie's coattails and benefit from the proprietary eponym—same shape, same smug little silhouette. But it has black ink and a green cap for some reason.

I don't even remember where it came from. It's as if it just appeared in the junk drawer one day, the way pens always do, as they crawl out of whatever void socks disappear into. It's much more likely I inadvertently stole it from a bank, or doctor's office, or some other place one encounters pens out in the wild.

Which means I am about to bring a human being into the world via a marker of unknown origin and unknown manufacture. Who knows where this fucking thing was before it found itself in my junk drawer.

I really should put more thought into the things I stick inside myself, not just from a metaphysical manifestation standpoint, but, like, a hygiene one.

My uterus contracts—not with "labor" or arousal, but with what I'm now willing to acknowledge is existential dread.

I don't know exactly how long I'm supposed to hold this marker in here, but I'm not ready to pull it out yet.

I could just pull it out.

I absolutely could.

I probably should…

But…I'm scared. Scared of what kind of person this marker is going to be. Because the last thing my life needs right now is another sentient manchild following me like I'm its mommy-slash-lover. *Freud would have a field day with us.*

I close my eyes, exhale slowly, and try to remember what it felt like to not be the golem-mother of inanimate objects with abandonment issues and the ability to marathon fuck me until my brain is incapable of coherent thought, let alone existential dread.

The marker gives a faint, uncomfortable twinge inside me.

Mom said I don't have to worry about the object transforming within me, but this thing is getting a life of its own, literally and metaphorically, because it's moving around inside me with what feels like impatience.

Not yet! I'm not ready!

Fuck. Fuck. Fuck.

My breath quickens. My chest tightens. My grip on the marker slips, and I think I might—yep, I'm having a panic attack.

Gage notices, puts down the cupcake he was sneakily eating, and drops to his knees beside me. He leans closer, eyes enormous and painfully sincere. "Alice," he says softly, "are you okay?"

I shift my hips, trying to find a position that doesn't jam cold plastic directly into my G-spot.

For a moment, I almost tell him the truth—that what would actually make me okay is someone taking care of me for once, not another sweet fuckboi pleasing me twenty-four-seven and making me omelets. But considering the circumstances, this marker is probably about to become another toddler with a robust cocktail of attachment disorders, and I just don't think I can handle that.

This kind of power is too much for an impulsive moron with the world's lowest standards.

My throat tightens.

Instead of telling him all that, I give him a small, wry smile.

The smile is apparently unconvincing, because he grabs my hand and asks, "Alice, is it too late to reconsider?"

The Sharpie is thrumming with a subsonic buzz that matches my favorite vibrator setting. I suppress the nostalgia it induces, but what I can't suppress is the static surging from my core and raising the hair on my arms, prickling my skin.

I feel a little high, a little floaty, like my body has been decoupled from the parts of my brain that handle consequences—if that coupling ever existed to begin with.

Shit. I'm running out of time. This thing is getting born whether I like it or not.

"Yes," I croak.

Reluctantly, I pull the marker out. It slides out slick and easy, as if my body is all too ready to be done with it.

I hold it up, and we both squint at it, inspecting it for changes.

Just a regular old marker—damp and radiating an aura of anticlimax.

Please, don't make me your mommy.

Be my zaddy.

CHAPTER 2
ALICE

The marker pulses, just a small heartbeat traveling the length of the plastic barrel, with a faint iridescent green glow, as I set it on the bed.

Gage, still kneeling at the edge of the bed, lowers to look closely at the marker. "Did I do this when you made me?"

"Pretty much, except you glowed blue," I say, pulling the comforter to cover my nudity, as a shiver runs through me.

As if mimicking me, the marker shivers, too. Then, without warning, it explodes.

Not violently. There's no gore, no ink or blood across the wall, just a sudden, solid mass of something dense and wrong, as if the universe switched to a different physics engine and the polygon mesh of the marker wasn't properly optimized for the new rules.

Gage shrieks—adorably, I might add—and falls back as the thing flies into the air.

The gooey, undulating mass lands with a soft, wet thud on the comforter before rolling onto the carpet.

For half a second, it's just a lump of inky wet topological wonder.

Then it moves.

It bulges outward in slow pulses, growing and collapsing, sprouting round protrusions that inflate like balloons and then collapse back into the mass before my brain can label them. One looks suspiciously like an elbow. Another like three knees banging together. Amongst the glowing globs of randomly exploding protuberances, the only one I am sure to make out is a penis—because, if I have any positive traits, it's my deeply unhelpful observational accuracy for spotting cock: *my cock-hawk-eye, if you will.*

Gage is back at my side, and we both watch, frozen in wonder and mild terror, as the assemblage splits open and a black fluid pours out, filling the air with the heavy, throat-closing scent of permanent ink.

The mass tightens—and then resolves.

A hand slips free. Pale. Slender. Precise. Masculine.

The fingers flex experimentally.

Another hand follows, and then—almost immediately—the rest of a man unfolds, not grown so much as *revealed*. He's kneeling on the carpet as if he'd been there all along, just waiting for this plane of existence to shift to the angle that would finally reveal him to us.

He plants one foot on the ground, rising slowly, as if gravity is a new but interesting concept. When he rises to his full height, he stretches and inhales deeply. He exhales a long, resonant "Haaaaaaaaah," and the iridescent glow encompassing him fades out with the word.

And now, he's just a man, standing there.

Gage and I just stare, our flabbers fully gasted.

He is not what I expected…not at all.

For one, he's fully dressed.

He looks as if he came from a universe where people are born ready for tenure-track. He's wearing an immaculate, slim-cut three-piece tweed suit with a navy tie, a crisp cream dress shirt, and leather shoes that gleam with a polished perfection that suggests they've never encountered a sidewalk or bad decision.

This is especially weird, considering Gage materialized completely naked. *Can they be born with clothes on?*

He's tall. Six feet, maybe a little more—*I'll ask Gage later.* Thin, but not fragile. The sort of build that suggests he has very strong opinions about literature and the core strength to defend them.

He's older than me. Well, in appearance anyway. He's only about

30, 40 seconds old, but he looks to be in his late thirties, early forties. His hair is thick, black, streaked dramatically with silver, as if…his hair were running out of black ink. *God, it's so on the nose, I wonder if Dionysus is also the god of lame dad jokes.*

His face has the same kind of offensively perfect composition that Gage's does. And in the same way Gage's eyes are an impossible blue, this guy's eyes are an impossible green. But unlike Gage's, which scream kindness and naivety, these look like they've spent years dissecting ideas with quiet contempt. All of that perfection is encased in a beard streaked black and white as intensely as his hair. *I've never considered myself a beard girl, but I think maybe I'm a beard girl.*

He glances down at himself, brushes invisible lint off his sleeve, and runs his hands through his hair in a way that expresses, "I'm going to ravish you, but, like, with emotional intelligence."

My brain is lagging behind the situation, flailing in the gap between expectation and reality. I was expecting someone more like Gage: young, hot, kinda dumb, sweet. But this guy is the amalgamation of every professor I ever had even the faintest of lady boners for. It's as if someone took every single one of their tingle-inducing traits, ramped them up to eleven, threw them into a blender, and then poured the concoction into the body of an actor portraying a professor on the big screen.

I want to say something, do anything, but when the man's eyes lock on me, the only thing I'm capable of is pulling the comforter close to my chest. I feel like I'm about to have my whole existence critiqued by an overly harsh art professor, and it is turning me on in a way I'm not sure I understand. As if his aesthetic wasn't lust-worthy enough, he reaches into his breast pocket to produce—*oh, God*—slutty fucking little glasses. He puts them on his face, and now I no longer think I'm being critiqued; I feel well and truly eye fucked.

Gage recovers first, stepping forward with his cupcakes and balloon in hand. "Welcome. I'm Gage. I used to be a blue ruler, but now I'm a man. You might remember me."

The marker, who is now an ultra-hot, kinda haughty human, doesn't even look at Gage. His gaze stays locked on me. He says, "Oh,

Alice," voice smooth and liquid, as he crosses the room and sits on the edge of the bed next to me, entirely at ease.

"Would you like a cupcake?" Gage asks, looking as deflated as a kōhai whose senpai didn't notice him.

Ignored.

The marker-man takes my hand, lifts it, and presses a slow, deliberate kiss to my knuckles. "Aren't you a sight for these newly acquired, sore eyes?" His smile curves—controlled, knowing, as if he's been practicing seduction in the mirror for decades.

"Uh, hi," I manage with a gulp.

"My name is Marc," he says. "Thank you for drawing me from the depths of inanimacy."

His whole aura is very specific.

Confident. Intelligent.

Professor. Poet. Problem.

Zaddy!

CHAPTER 3
ALICE

Marc presses another kiss to my knuckles and says, "Oh, this hand. I've longed to hold it, as it once held me." With his free hand, he strokes the hair out of my eye. "Thank you, my lovely. This body you've given me is remarkable. You are a true artist."

Marc hasn't stopped smiling at me since his birth-slash-personification. The air is thick with the smell of ink, magic residue, and this man's heady, bewildering scent—it's how I suspect sexual knowledge in APA format would smell. *I know that makes no sense, hence why I said "bewildering."* The combination has seduced me into absolute submission.

"I—uh—I didn't do much," I stammer.

He smirks and moves closer. "Nonsense. I didn't appear from thin air. I was drawn here by intention: yours. Your deepest desires, even the ones you aren't fully aware of."

Gage, still holding the "Welcome!" balloon and his tray of Funfetti cupcakes, hovers behind Marc, looking more lost than I've ever seen him—and dude gets lost a lot. He shifts and clears his throat, but Marc's attention is unwavering—laser-focused on me.

It's the type of attention that makes me feel all gooey inside. I try to speak, but it comes out as a croak.

Marc leans in, face so close I can't focus. His voice drops so low I can feel it vibrate through the bones of my pelvis. "Forgive my forwardness, Alice. My memory is a cluster of impressions and sensations: all of them you. I must kiss you." He says it like he's asking permission to critique my manuscript, not invade my face, but technically, he didn't ask permission to do that either.

He kisses me before I can respond. His lips are cool and insistent, tongue tracing the seam of my mouth like he's scribing poetry on my palate.

I make a small, involuntary noise that I hope sounds like assent and not the dying gasp of a startled ferret.

When he pulls back, he looks at me with honest yearning. "I'm here to take care of you, Alice." He reaches for the comforter I'm gripping at my chin.

I flinch.

He pauses and asks, "Are you afraid of me?"

I swallow. "Should I be?"

"I'd rather dry up than hurt you," he replies, meeting my eyes.

Once again, he doesn't wait for a response before he proceeds. He pulls the comforter from my grasp and slowly peels it away, exposing my body—pantless and pantiless, covered only by a t-shirt. A t-shirt with a fan-service-y anime character on it, because the occasion I dressed for was definitely not this one.

When the cold air hits my exposed pussy, my legs snap shut, and my knees pull to my chest, as my arms wrap around them.

His fingers catch my jaw and tilt my face up. "Oh, my lovely. You're exquisite. You should never hide."

He doesn't have to pry me back open; he simply touches my arms, and they fall to my side. He slides his palm between my knees, spreading me, running his hand down my leg as he admires the newly unobstructed sight of me.

"You could say I've spent my entire existence inside you," he growls, "and it's a little difficult adjusting to the distance." His voice rumbles, velvet and steel—or maybe hard plastic.

He slips a finger inside me, slick, confident, declaring, "The first thing I knew was your warmth. The first thing I felt was your desire."

I moan and arch into his touch.

He whispers, voice now breathy and relieved, "Your sacred center is the origin of creation."

He curls his finger inside me, moaning as he caresses my walls. His other hand braces my shoulder, pinning me to the headboard.

I whimper, biting my lower lip and closing my eyes.

"You held me in here longer than necessary," he whispers. "Now all I want is to dive back in."

He slips in another finger, then leans close to my ear, "Tell me what you want." His fingers curl inside me again, pressing hard as his thumb finds my clit.

I gasp, then open my eyes to admit, "I want someone to take care of me for once," grinding upward to meet his thumb.

His laugh is low and gentle. "Oh, baby, I can definitely do that."

He grips the back of my head and pulls me into a kiss. His fingers increase their pressure inside me, pumping harder. His thumb circles more firmly, more methodically.

I tilt my hips, grinding down, already chasing orgasm.

Gage makes a strangled noise, and Marc stops, finally looking at him.

Fuck. I had forgotten Gage was here.

I blink. "Oh—Marc, this is Gage."

Marc regards Gage as one would a cheap wine. "Ah. The former measuring stick."

Gage flushes. "That's—me?"

Marc's attention returns to me. "Why is he here?"

"He's my boyfriend," I say.

"Oh," Marc replies, emotionless, and leans in to nibble my neck. "I don't mind if the boy watches me fuck you."

Gage and I freeze, our gaze locked on each other, both unsure what to say or do.

Marc pulls back, studying my face, then following my eyes to Gage's. He pulls back, fingers still inside me, stroking slowly, and says to Gage, "Gage, was it?"

Gage nods excitedly. "Yes, Gage." He thrusts the balloon and cupcakes forward. "Welcome!"

The balloon sways, careening toward Marc's face. Before it hits him, Marc removes the hand pinning me to the headboard and jabs upward, puncturing the balloon with a marker, then returns an empty hand to my shoulder.

Gage leaps backward, with another cute yelp.

I startle, as well, clenching around Marc's fingers, deftly exploring my innards.

"Sorry," Marc says, perfectly unrepentant, "it was distracting."

Gage looks as deflated as the balloon.

Marc sighs, looks between Gage and me again, and a decision crosses his face, softening it. He turns back to Gage and says with a shrug, "I suppose I can fuck you, too, if that is what Alice wants."

Marc leans in, returning his mouth's attention to my neck, my ear, and increasing the pressure on my clit. "Is that what you want, baby? You want me to fuck both of you?"

My brain flickers on, then off, then on again, while an old-school slideshow flashes increasingly lewd combinations of our bodies through my imagination. I gasp, "Yes."

"Come here," Marc commands.

Gage, good boy that he is, obeys. Entranced, he sets the cupcake tray aside and stands beside us.

CHAPTER 4
ALICE

Marc's fingers continue to curl inside me, while he unbuttons his fly. I catch a flash of striped navy and emerald boxer-briefs as he produces the most intimidating cock I have ever seen, and I am dating a man whose dick is literally a foot long.

It's not the size. It's the bearing. The composure.

Marc's cock is stately, dignified, the sort of dick that knows the difference between "farther" and "further" and will pound the knowledge into you over and over and over until you know, too.

It's not just a cock; it's a syllabus. It's office hours. It's a midterm you didn't study for, and now it's going to teach you a lesson you'll never forget by bending you over a knee.

It's longer than average, but not cartoonish—*like some people I know.* But the design: that's what's intimidating. It's exquisitely symmetrical, uncircumcised, with a shaft so perfectly ridged it's as if it were sculpted to maximize both sensation and aesthetics. When my eyes rake over it, I can practically feel those ridges raking inside me. The thing stands so proper, so regal, the crown might as well be wearing a little mortarboard to go with its foreskin robe.

Gage is silent, eyes wide, mouth slightly agape, his own dick at full mast, straining against the constraints of his sweatpants. The look on his face says he's maybe doing that "calibrating" thing, as he, too, realizes this is the dick you measure all other dicks against.

I open my mouth to do what I always do when I'm feeling intimidated: make a joke or suck a cock. But Marc cuts me off when he removes his fingers crooking inside me, and says, "Come," crooking them outside me, effectively cutting off all plans I had of making decisions for myself.

I come. Well, I move toward him. I haven't come yet.

He pulls me, bodily, onto his lap, aligning me with his cock. I try to say something witty about how this is very sudden, but he's already guiding the head against me, blunt and demanding, and the words evacuate my mouth all at once in a gasp.

He pushes the head in with a slow, confident motion, splitting me open in increments. With each push, he lets the stretch settle before he slides deeper, punctuating each increment with what sounds a lot like poetry.

He murmurs in my ear, "Before I had a body."

Deeper. "I had ache."

Deeper. "I had longing."

Deeper. "For you."

Deeper. "Always for you."

It's not rushed. It's not even rough.

It's deliberate. Every moment, every word, crafted to make my whole body vibrate.

It's perfect, and I am devouring every moment of it.

He sheathes himself fully with a final thrust, and I nearly black out from the pleasure when he hits me deep and thick.

He's not done pontificating, but I don't mind, because he says, "My whole existence was marked by the moments you enveloped me in your grip. Used me. And now…" he moans, closing his eyes and tilting his head back. "I can wrap you around me the way I've always wanted."

With a sudden, almost dismissive gesture, he peels my shirt over my head, leaving me bare. "Beautiful, my darling."

He kisses me again before he pulls back to place my nipple in his mouth. He flicks his tongue and sucks, moaning as if the act brings him the same pleasure it brings me.

My hips move of their own accord, rolling against him, greedy for friction.

With his mouth still full of me, Marc looks to Gage, who is watching intently, mouth hanging open hungrily, fists balled at his side, and dick begging to be included.

Marc breaks the suction with a wet pop, leaving my nipple shiny and a little swollen. "Gage," he commands, not looking away from me, "take off your clothes," before returning his mouth to me.

Gage hesitates, glances at me for approval.

I nod—fuck, I'm nodding so hard I might snap my own neck.

Gage starts with his t-shirt, pulling it over his head, revealing the kind of abs you only get from being manifested from the imagination of a complete and utter perv. He drops his sweatpants and underwear in one go, and his cock springs free: comically, beautifully huge, as always, but now it's being graded against a new rubric.

He shuffles closer, standing at the edge of the bed, every inch of him at attention, pointing right at Marc's face.

Marc turns, looking at the part of Gage no one can ignore. He grins at the sight and asks, "Twelve inches, I presume?"

Gage looks shyly pleased. "Precisely," he says in that adorably perfunctory way he does that makes his cock bob just a little.

"Pulchritudinous," Marc declares, with a sigh, as if he's reluctantly awarding extra credit, then buries his face between my breasts.

I can't help myself: "What the fuck does that mean?"

Marc looks up at me, resting his chin on my breastbone. "It's the longest word in the English language for beautiful. It felt…" he exhales as if exasperated with himself, "fitting." He shrugs. "I thought the boy would appreciate praise of his length with a word of length."

Gage's entire body blushes bright red, confirming Marc's suspicions.

Marc licks my nipple again, then tugs me up, turning me around so my back is pressed against his chest, legs splayed wide, pussy still full of his cock.

Marc manhandles me, leaning me toward Gage's cock. Then whispers, breath hot and sweet, "Go ahead, Alice. Take him in your mouth." He leans me forward more. "Let me see that beautiful mouth around that beautiful cock."

I lean the remaining distance, steadying myself with a hand on Gage's hip. He is already leaking, and a drop glistens at the tip. I lick it up, making him whimper.

"That's a good girl. Now take him," Marc says, kissing my neck.

I run my tongue up the underside of Gage's cock, tracing the vein with my tongue, the way I know he likes, then take him in as far as I can into my mouth.

It's still absurd how big Gage's dick is. I manage maybe half before my gag reflex protests. I pop off, take a deep breath, and try again, swirling my tongue around the head before working my way back down.

Behind me, Marc begins to move, slow at first, rocking his hips up so his cock slides in and out of me in perfect time with the movement of my mouth on Gage.

Gage's hands float at his sides, unsure what to do. I grab one and place it on my head, and he immediately gets the message, threading his fingers through my hair and gently guiding me onto his cock.

Marc's hand slides between my thighs, circling my clit with that same deliberate, controlled pressure as before. He pinches my nipple with the other hand at the exact moment he bites my ear.

I'm the filling in a fuck sandwich, and all I can do is moan around the cock in my mouth.

Marc nibbles at my neck, whispering praise as he kisses me. "That's my girl. Look at you taking our cocks so well."

Every word builds me higher and closer to climax.

He praises Gage, too. "That's a good boy. Give it to her, just like that. Oh, look at you two. Marvelous."

With each word, Gage moans, clenching his thighs and pushing just a little deeper down my throat.

Marc must like to hear himself talk just as much as Gage and I do, because he doesn't let up. "Oh, baby, you feel so fucking good. Thank you for giving me this cock." He picks up the pace, his fingers working my clit faster, his cock pounding up into me, nearly bucking me off his lap. The wet slap of flesh almost drowns out the obscene noises I'm making around Gage's dick.

Gage is making little mewling noises, like he's about to cry from how good it feels. He always does this when I suck his cock, and it is the hottest thing I've ever witnessed.

Marc's voice in my ear: "You like being taken care of, baby? Show my cock how good you're being taken care of. Let me feel those walls flutter, baby."

I try to say "Yes," but my mouth is full. Instead, I hum, and the vibration makes Gage's knees buckle.

Gage's reaction is the force that breaks the dam holding back my orgasm. I come so hard I see stars, my whole body spasming, and my scream vibrating around Gage's cock, the pleasure rushing out of me and destroying everything around me.

Gage stops thrusting, letting me ride out the orgasm as I suck him harder. But Marc continues his assault on my pussy, nearly shouting for joy, "That's it. That's my good girl. Come for us, baby." The world collapses to a pinpoint of sensation, and then slowly expands back out, leaving me limp and shaking in Marc's arms, with the head of Gage's cock resting against my cheek.

I'm a puddle, boneless, eyes dropping closed, ready to sleep, when Marc kisses my cheek next to Gage's cock, saying, "You can't sleep yet, baby. We're not done with you. This only marks the beginning of our experience."

Neither of them have come—part of being a sex-golem is never coming first, I suppose. So I didn't for a second think these two were done fucking me.

CHAPTER 5
GAGE

Marc shifts Alice from his lap to the bed, dangling her legs over the edge. He places his hand on my shoulder and says, "Show me you know how to use that cock." He smacks my ass and pushes me toward the bed—toward Alice. "Fuck her properly. Like a good boy."

I'm so flustered by being called "good boy" that I forget where my center of balance is and fall forward. I catch myself before I fall onto Alice, but my cock nudges her slick entrance.

She spreads wide for me, but I look at Marc, hoping for direction.

It's not that I don't know what to do. I was literally made to do this. But for some reason, I need him to tell me how to do it.

Marc smirks, rolls his eyes, and says, "Go ahead. Fill that pussy for me."

Alice wraps her arms around my neck, pulling me forward, and I slide in easily, sheathing my dick in its home.

The feeling is, as always, overwhelming, but with Marc here, watching us both, it's like every inch of me gliding into her is a full frontal attack on my already-overstimulated, recently-assembled nervous system.

Alice is also oversensitive; each inch of me makes her shake and whine. "Oh, Gage. Oh, God."

Marc stands beside the bed, hands on his hips, eyes locked on the place where my body meets Alice's. "That's it. Deeper," he says.

I surge forward until my hips are flush against her ass; the motion is so intense that I nearly come. I close my eyes tight, doing anything I can not to, because I can't disappoint Alice—I can't disappoint Marc—by coming so quickly.

Alice arches her back and moans, screaming in that way she always does when I bottom out into her.

Marc leans over and brushes her hair back from her face, then kisses her forehead like a reward. "You're doing very well, Alice," he purrs, then turns to me. "And you, too, Gage. You're giving her everything you have. Now make her come."

The validation does something to me.

Before I know it, I'm fucking Alice harder, deeper, just as he instructs, until she's clawing at the bedsheets and her cunt is spasming around my shaft, milking me, and she's screaming louder than I have ever heard her scream during an orgasm.

I'm beaming down at the beauty that is 'Alice coming because of me,' when Marc makes a noise of impatience.

My smile falls as I watch him cross the room, unbuttoning his jacket.

Did I do something wrong? Did I do it too fast? Too slow?

He shrugs off his jacket in one fluid motion, folding it neatly over his arm.

Alice clenches around my cock, cooing with sleepy satisfaction.

Marc pauses at the mess that is Alice's clothing 'storage system'—a chair for clean clothes and a floor for everything else—and places his blazer atop the rim of the chair.

He turns, notices me watching him, and chastises, "Keep going. Don't stop."

I look down at Alice; she's boneless, languid on the bed, dazed and smiling, but still wrapped around my cock. She's got that look on her face I've come to know and love: the look that says, "I'm so fucked out, you better not move or touch me or I'm gonna hit you."

I turn back to Marc, ready to protest, even though I'm kind of scared to, but he's standing naked at my side, and my words freeze in my throat at the sight of him.

Alice sits up, her bones now returned to her body, and gapes along with me.

Black ink covers every inch of him as if someone drew all over his body with a Sharpie. *Gods, Alice is right, we sex golems are overly literal creatures.*

And every square inch of ink has one unifying theme: Alice, making his entire body a canvas dedicated to her.

Her name is repeated in numerous styles: from elegant script to blocky graffiti to jagged urgency. It's not just her name, though. It's also her. Parts of her, all of her, scattered across his body: a portrait over his heart, her profile along his ribs, her eyes watching from his shoulders, her lips on his forearm, her spread pussy on his thigh. Even his toes spell ALICE across them. The only parts of him not covered in a rendering of her are his hands, face, and genitals.

Marc stands, unashamed, his devotion literally inscribed on his flesh.

I want to ask about the tattoos, but before I can, Marc is at my back, one hand on my shoulder, the other bracing his weight against my back. "Keep fucking her," he instructs, voice low and close to my ear. "Leave your mark inside her, baby boy."

I'm trembling, not from fear, at least I don't think it is. It's a feeling completely new to me, *but most are…*

Surprisingly, Alice doesn't comment on the tattoos—all sarcasm and wit removed from her and replaced by a feral ferocity. She pulls me into a kiss so fierce it short-circuits my ability to be self-conscious.

Marc stays at my back. He grips my hips firmly, guiding my body, thrusting me inside of her. He sets a rhythm, guiding me forward and back, slow at first, then harder, faster. It's like he's using me to fuck her in exactly the way he wants, while pressing his weight against my back, blocking my escape—not that I want to escape.

Alice moans into my mouth, then breaks away to pant in my ear. "God, Gage, you feel so good, I'm gonna—fuck—I can't even—"

Marc's hands leave my hips and begin exploring my body. One slides upward, stopping to squeeze my pec, and the other slides to the space between Alice and me, pressing below my belly button. "Don't hold back. Give her all of it. Give her everything you've got."

I do. I slam into her, and Alice falls backward onto the bed, dragging me down with her.

I keep thrusting, steady and deep. Alice is squeezing me so tight I'm not sure I'll make it, but I want to make Marc proud.

I want him to tell me I'm a good boy again.

CHAPTER 6
GAGE

Marc's hand slides down my spine, then cups my ass, thumb digging in just where the curve crests. He glides to the center of me, then spreads me open. His mouth is on my neck, breath hot in my ear, when he places a small kiss behind it.

His thumb presses forward and I freeze. "You remember, don't you?" he whispers, circling right at the opening of my asshole.

I don't respond. I don't even breathe.

"Don't slow. She's going to come soon," Marc says, voice soft and approving, as he returns his hands to my hips, guiding me to thrust inside Alice again.

Alice is digging crescents into my biceps. Her thighs are trembling around my hips, and her feet are scrabbling for purchase on the mattress.

He's right.

I continue my rhythm, my innate need to please sexually outweighing any fear I may have.

Marc's hands slide from my hips up my tailbone, tracing my spine. "Tell me you remember. Tell me. Back when we were in the drawer together," he says as he outlines my crack, not yet reaching back in.

My brain scrambles to recall my time before it even existed—when I was still a ruler.

He whispers into my ear. "Come on, Gage. You remember when I would rest in your divot."

"My what?"

"The channel. The ruler groove. Your little…slit." Marc's voice is a hot current right through me, spreading the recollection of our shared history in the junk drawer through my whole body, as he spreads my cheeks again.

The memory is there—well, not the memory, but the impression. The knowing. Something every cell in my body didn't experience, but somehow retains. Endless, quiet hours in the drawer. Marker and ruler pressed together in the dark.

He strokes a finger down my cleft.

"Yes," I gasp, as my cock twitches inside Alice. "I…I remember."

"Sometimes I'd be wedged in there for days. Then Alice would use me and put me right back in my resting place." His finger encircles my anus. "Right where I fit. Right where I belonged." He says it so matter-of-factly, so sincerely, that it sounds more sweet than lewd.

"Was that why you wanted me to be brought to life?" Marc asks, his voice gentle, breathy. "So you could put me back inside you?"

I freeze. The question is so raw I feel like I'm being assessed, grilled—probed—tested with a single-question pop quiz, and I have a 50% chance of failing.

"Don't stop, Gage," Alice wails, and I pick my pace back up, unable to concentrate on her, because I'm still trying to answer Marc's question—not just for him, but for myself.

Is that what I want? Is that why I asked Alice to bring him to life?

Did I want—do I want—to be filled by him again? Not as a ruler, but as a man?

I look at Alice for help, but her eyes are gone, rolled up in ecstatic white; she's not going to tell me what to do. And, honestly, in this state, she'll just tell me to "get fucked"—like in the good way, not in the insult way.

Marc awaits my response patiently, but his fingers aren't patient. One presses lightly at my entrance, rushing my response.

My answer is a whimper and a thrust backward.

"Say it," Marc growls into my ear, finger never leaving its post. "Tell me why you wanted me here."

The truth is: *yes, I want to be filled by Marc.* The thought is so electric a tremor pulses through my cock, making Alice gasp.

I can barely form words, but I manage to choke out, "Because I wanted you to fill me."

"That's a good boy," he says, pressing his finger in just enough to make the world narrow to the tightness of Alice squeezing my cock, the velvet heat of Marc's breath, and the swirl of sensation inside me. It's all so intense it blots out everything else.

"Wait," I stammer, "shouldn't we—do we need lube?"

Marc laughs, deep and happy. "Oh, Gage. I haven't dried out yet. Thanks to you." He brings his hand forward so I can see his fingers glistening with a faintly green, shimmering fluid.

"One of my powers," Marc says, and returns his hand to my ass. He presses a finger in—so slick, so wet, so smooth, so perfect.

I gasp, then whimper.

Alice clenches around me in response.

He rolls within me, slow and insistent, gaining depth.

I can't help but rut into Alice harder, as if putting on a show for him.

I want him to see how good I am at this. How good I can make Alice feel. How good he makes me feel.

He preps me with another finger, then another, maybe another, I can't tell. It's so wet and so gentle and increasing in a way that seems to meet every craving my body has.

But his fingers aren't all I crave. I also crave his approval, his praise. He feeds me that, too. "You're doing so well, Gage. Such a good boy."

I melt, falling apart from the overload of it and pumping into Alice like the brain she built for me has left my body.

Then, his fingers pull out of me, and something new is pressing against my entrance: his dick.

Marc grips my hips again and says, "You are remarkable, Gage. You're going to take all of me, right?"

He doesn't wait for my response, which, even if given time, I probably couldn't have given him anyway. The only parts of me working right now are below the waist.

He pushes in, slow, deliberate, unyielding.

The world goes white.

I cry out. It doesn't hurt. Not really. But the sensation is overwhelming.

Marc hushes me, soothing, "Easy. Take it. There you go. That's my good boy."

He pushes a little more.

A little more.

A little more until I finally relax and let him in even more.

His cock is a miracle. It finds every nerve ending and pushes them all at once.

And now he's fully inside me.

He gives me time—waits for me to push back.

I do.

And when I do, he drags back, then pushes forward.

At first, it's the shock of invasion, and then the bloom of pleasure, as he moves in time with my thrusts into Alice.

He leans over me, mouth at my ear. "You're doing so well," he says, and I almost believe it.

But my brain seems to have returned to my body and resumes its usual reeling of irrepressible, anxious thoughts that have nagged me since I saw the way Alice looked at his cock.

Marc is so good. He's so much better at all of this.

I can't measure up to him.

I'm just a dick. He's a dick and smooth talk.

He can make her scream with only 7.32 inches. He can make me beg.

What can I do? Not that.

Even his sex golem power is cooler than mine: self-lubricating. All I can do is grow a measuring tape out of my hand and get hard whenever someone so much as looks at me funny.

I feel like I'm fading, even as I'm being filled.

Marc must sense it, because he slows down, pulls me up by the shoulders, and wraps his arm around my chest, kissing me hard on the temple. "Hey, baby boy. You measure up. I promise. You feel so good. And look at her. You're doing that, not me."

Alice is clawing at my back with her legs clamped at my side. She gasps, "I love you, Gage."

I lean in to kiss her, then say, "I love you, too, Alice."

Marc gives us our moment before he says, "You made this possible, Gage. I'd still be in the drawer if it weren't for you. You saved me. You're a good friend."

I want to protest, but he starts fucking me again, leaning me forward with a hand braced at my lower back, thrusting so hard into me I could be a puppet he's fucking Alice with.

The pleasure drowns out my words. It silences my internal monologue of self-doubt.

Marc's rhythm becomes erratic, and he growls, "Come for me, Gage. Come for Alice. Fill her up for me while I draw all over your back."

I can't hold back.

I slam into Alice, again and again, until I explode inside her, and every one of my muscles locks.

Alice comes with me, bucking and shaking.

And just when I think I'm done coming, a second orgasm explodes within me from Marc's thrusts inside me. I wail and fall forward onto Alice's breasts. She hugs my head as I twitch and convulse.

And just when I think I can't take it anymore, Marc pulls out, shooting his load across my back.

CHAPTER 7
MARC

I lie on my back, between them, staring at the ceiling. There's a hairline crack running directly above the length of me...

The ceiling mocks me.
When will my facade crack, too?
Will they still love me?

It's almost too fucking poetic...even for me.

Gage is draped over my chest. His head is nestled in the hollow beneath my collarbone, and his cock is flopped over my thigh like a spent eel. Alice is on my other side, curled into the crescent of my arm, tracing the letters of her name between my ribs.

Alice sighs, "Jesus Christ. I think I came more times today than when Gage first appeared." She says it as an idle fact, like one of the notes she'd write with me. She might as well have said, "Dentist appointment, 3:00 p.m., March 31. Brush your teeth beforehand. I came eight times on Marc's cock." She is not commenting on Gage's sexual prowess, or mine even, just making an observation.

But Gage stiffens, anyway.

It's minuscule—a fractional tensing of his neck muscles, a micro-twitch of his jaw, a ripple of inadequacy so brief it barely registers.

But I see it. I am, after all, designed to see it.

I glide a hand up his back and squeeze, to remind him that he is, in fact, being held. He is safe here in my arms. I am here to take care of him and Alice. "Well, this time he had a little help," I say, pitching my voice low and warm, and rubbing my cheek on his crown.

Alice snorts. "The phrase 'back blown out' is starting to feel a lot less metaphoric and a lot more literal to me." She grinds her wet center on my leg.

My cock, once again, goes as rigid as the plastic my body once was—ready to be used by her.

Gage, like my dick, shoots up, "We have hurt your back?" He says it as both a statement and a question.

Alice strokes his face, "No, babe, it's still a metaphor."

He relaxes and returns to his resting place on my shoulder.

Alice rubs her lower back, and it's apparent she is actually in pain, just hiding it for his sake. I rub it for her, and she smiles up at me in silent thanks.

She laughs, "So, I know technically I've got so much sex golem DNA inside my lineage, I might as well be one, too, but I am going to have trouble keeping up with the two of you."

I'm not sure I like being called a "sex golem." I almost protest and say I prefer to be called a 'transmundane manifestation of desire, bestowed upon an inanimate object by a celestial super power and vaginal rugae.' I'd even settle for 'cosmically crafted companion chimera.' But it's obviously some inside joke they share, and I can't fight it without blowing my cool and collected cover.

I smirk. "That's fine, darling. We can wear each other out for you," I say, squeezing Gage close to me, wondering if I can actually keep up with him. Yes, I am newly made, but my body does seem to feel the age it was gifted.

"I only want to make you both happy. I don't need to be worn out…unless you want to wear me out," Gage says, muffled by my chest, the words buzzing against my sternum.

My chest tightens.

Alice and Gage poured so much of their hope in me when I was materializing. They're starving for approval, affection, and constant, relentless reassurance. I am supposed to be the well from which they pull their ink—a daddy, a zaddy, a solid, unwavering hand at the small of their backs.

I rub both of their backs, and they nuzzle into me.

But I am not a daddy.

I am a marker whose once half-empty reservoir is now overfilled with performance anxiety, as he puts a cap on his true desires.

The moment my body materialized, I felt it: a gravitational pull to the center of this triad, a need to orchestrate and control, an urge to keep the peace and pleasure perfectly on point.

I am the ultrafine tip that must balance his straight edge, while I'm held in her unsteady, chaotic grip.

I fake a stretch to cover the spike of panic and sit as if to leave, even though I don't really know where to go.

"That's the bathroom over there," Alice says, pointing at a door.

Bathroom? What is that?

Gage sits up. "Peeing for the first time is really weird. Just like, point it into the bowl." He grabs his dick, pointing it downward. "It's like cumming, but also not. It helps to turn on the faucet. The water helps your brain work out what needs to happen. Alice's dad taught me that trick."

I pretend to know what the fuck he's talking about. "Thanks, but I got it," I say coolly and walk toward the door, hoping that I don't walk like a guy who just learned how to do it, which I am.

I enter the room that's supposed to hold baths, but I see none as I close the door behind me.

I look up and am startled by a man covered in backward tattoos of Alice. I surge forward to fight him, for sullying her name thusly, when I realize…it's just me.

I grip the counter and stare at my reflection.

Fuck, is this really what I look like?

How the fuck am I supposed to maintain this daddy facade when I'm literally wearing a fucking heart with Alice's name in it on my sleeve?

I review the markings on my body: all devoted to Alice, which makes sense; she is the center of my universe—always has been.

I lean against the wall and inspect my body. I know a little bit about how this thing works, thanks to the magic that made me and Alice's perversely adorable compulsion to draw dicks on things with me—dicks that sometimes came with full bodies.

Barrel replaced by body.
Beating heart.
Breathing lungs.
Barely and fully human.

My breath quickens, and I feel the same way I know Alice did when she was building me: panicked.

This is not the man I wanted to be. Not at all.

When she held me inside her, flowing her magic into me, my first conscious thought was, "Oh, my love. I thought your hand grip was divine, but the grip of these walls is transcendent." Until that moment, my greatest wish had been to experience her right hand around me, but that all changed as she gave me life. New desires began to materialize along with me.

I was going to show her how good I am at helping her remember things—*fuck post-its, we don't need them when we have each other.*

I was going to spend my days drawing, writing poetry, and finally tasting Thai food. I've written dates on so many Thai food containers, it must be the pinnacle of human culinary achievement.

But right as my body began to take shape, she wished so hard it ripped the fabric of the reality weaving within me.

I knew exactly what to do. I became what she needed.

A cosmic drive to be inside her again steered me right to her. *A puppet. A 'sex golem' controlled by some celestial power—or maybe instinct. Same difference?*

But then the strings were cut, and I had free will. And that's when I saw him.

And I knew I needed to be what he needed, too.

They need someone to hold them together.

They need a steady hand…but how can I be that, when a steady hand is what I've always needed myself?

I spot a white roll of paper and, without thinking, grab the empty air. A marker slides into my grip—green-capped, unbranded, and green-inked, the way I was long, long, long ago.

Before…

Before…

Even as a marker, I pretended to be someone I was not.

I close my eyes.

I can still feel the parts of me that weren't granted life. My original green ink barrel rots, fully desiccated, under a refrigerator. The black cap of the barrel I ultimately claimed lies crushed at the back of my old drawer, providing refuge for a lone paperclip and pushpin.

I look at my hands.

If this body still had its original cap, would it be easier to be what Alice needs?

My hand shakes as I uncap the marker, the scent comforting, chemical, nostalgic.

I scrawl upon the snow-white paper. The words spill out, not neatly, not with the calligrapher's hand I once dreamed of mastering, but ragged and desperate and raw:

My soft-felt tip must harden if I am to be permanent.
I mustn't dry out.
Ink that once bled. Replaced by flesh that does the same. Equally undesirable.
I must leave a mark that will not fade from their hearts.
Alice—smeared.
Gage—smudged.
Marc—truth redacted.
Uncapped promise—indelible.
Unremarkable.

CHAPTER 8
MARC

I must have spent more time in the bathroom than is customary because I emerge to Gage and Alice whispering with concern written all over their faces.

Alice props herself up on an elbow. "Marc, are you okay?"

My heart stops—which I'm assuming is a bad thing. I'm grateful for the hair on my face, as it helps to hide my expressions.

"Of course," I say, swaggering into the room. "I'm always good. That's how you made me."

I slide between them, reclaiming my spot.

Alice remains suspicious. Her eyes bore into me, and I'm not sure if I have a soul, but if I do, she's seeing right through to it. "No one is always good."

Gage, from behind, nuzzles into the nape of my neck. "You don't have to be perfect, Marc. Being human is hard."

I close my eyes, letting their warmth radiate into me, wishing I could believe what they say.

But I am not allowed to fuck up. Not here. Not with them. Not now.

I am the line that guides them.

I must be a steady hand.

If my resolve fades, if I reveal my true feelings, their love will dissolve…

My feelings are not important. So, it's best just not to discuss them.

I wrap my arms around them both. "I appreciate your concern, but there is no need to worry about me. Just getting used to this body. That peeing thing took longer than I suspected."

A look crosses between them that makes me think they know I didn't do whatever peeing is.

Before they can challenge me further, I grab Alice by the ass, hoisting her so that she sits on my dick. "Shall we continue fucking, my love?"

Alice presses her hands into my chest. "No. Let's talk. Let's get to know each other," she says, stretching her arms over her head so that her whole body bows with the effort.

The sight is so beautiful that my dick rises without any direction from me. When it nestles between her ass cheeks, my hand slicks, ready to lube her so that I may enter her, but she moves to the side and says, "Can we talk about the tattoos now?"

"Which tattoos?" I ask, feigning innocence.

She sits up, suddenly, cross-legged, view impeccable. "All of them. Any of them. Why are you covered in…me?"

Gage adds, "You have Alice written on you in at least 117 unique ways. Every body part is represented at least 3 different ways. Her hand has the most representations. There are 9 renderings of her left hand and 8 of her right."

Gage's precision is both impressive and deeply inconvenient.

"You missed the one hidden under my balls," I say, deadpan, and wink at Gage. "Care to get a closer look?"

Alice pulls away, not annoyed but not yielding, either. "You didn't answer the question."

Because I need you to know I am yours.

I need you to know I have more than enough ink.

I shrug. "You made me this way."

She doesn't buy the answer.

I don't know how to explain it without exposing a core I don't want touched.

She wants a poet. She wants an artist. She wants a man devoted to caring for her. She wants confident and calm.

So I smirk, stretch my arms overhead, and say, "Because, darling, you're my muse. My inspiration. My reason for existing, quite literally. We're drawn together by fate."

Alice smiles, flattered, but she's not letting it go. "Yeah, but why is it all over your body? Gage feels the same way, but he's not covered in tattoos."

I want to tell her the truth. That the idea of her forgetting me, not remembering I belong to her, discarding me, opens a pit in what I presume is my heart so black it makes the ink on my body look white.

I want to say I think Dionysus is mocking me. Punishing me for my lack of transparency as a marker…

I almost answer. Almost. But my feelings are not important.

I spread my hands, making a show of it. "I'm an artist. You're my muse. I was a marker, and now I'm a marked man. It's not that deep." It comes out too fast, too glib.

Alice doesn't look convinced, but she lets it drop. She reaches out and runs her thumb over the Alice on my wrist. "This one is my favorite," she says, wistfully.

I want to ask her why, but I know it would lead her to expect me to name my favorite. I can't.

They are all the same. They are all her. They are all perfect.

There is no best. *There is only constant, relentless wanting.*

I want to be used. I want to be yours permanently.

Gage says, "I think the one on your thigh is best. Very anatomical." He flushes, tracing the pussy inked next to my cock.

I clap him on the back, which nearly knocks him off the bed. "See. Gage gets it. A perfect pussy like that must be immortalized." I laugh.

Gage's gaze remains fixed on my thigh. "Do you remember being a marker?" he asks.

I look at my hands, the elegant length of my fingers, the slight webbing at the base of my thumb. The perfection that's not quite human. "I remember…the darkness. The drawer."

My face begins to burn unpleasantly, and I stop myself from sinking into the darkness of my mind. I try to sound less melancholy and more manly. "I remember the heat of her hand. The pressure. The way she gripped me."

I remember wanting. Wanting more. Wanting you. Wanting to be used.

My words are getting too close to the inky core of me. So, I finish with a more neutral topic: "I remember every date on every takeout container."

Alice's face softens. "Were you lonely?"

Yes. Always. Except when you used me.

I look at her, at Gage, and I want to say, "Of course I was." But I don't want to admit it, not even to myself. So I say, "I was a marker. We do not feel such things."

Alice lets the saving silence hang, but then asks, "So what's the story with the green cap? Do you know why you had the incorrect cap?"

Incorrect cap…

The words punch me in the sternum.

The air shifts, cold and sharp.

Memories overfill me. A thousand blurry moments of being held, uncapped, used, recapped, discarded, rolling in the drawer under the weight of other objects.

For months—years—I was nothing but a vessel for someone else's mark.

A tale of two markers.
One relied on to remember.
One favored for fun.
Cap broken. Can't dry out—too important. Can't forget.
Cap stolen. Dried out. Unnecessary. Lost. Forgotten.

I can't look at her.

I can't look at him.

I lie back, feigning nonchalance, but my eyes catch the ceiling crack that I am sure Dionysus created just to mock me.

The gods are cruel, after all.

I want to tell them the truth of me—of my marker merger. I want to confess. But if I do, I know what happens next.

You don't keep the marker that's no longer useful. You toss it and buy a new one.

Maybe drying out, being discarded, would be better than the constant fear of it.

Alice is waiting.

Gage is waiting.

I open my mouth to say something, anything, but the words clot in my throat.

The room is silent except for their hope, and my fear, and the faint, almost imperceptible buzzing in my head that grows louder the longer I don't answer.

Mercifully, the buzz in my head is accompanied by a buzz of Alice's phone on the nightstand.

She throws herself across Gage and me, reaching for it, her nudity pressed perfectly against us.

CHAPTER 9
ALICE

I don't even have to look at the phone to know it's my mother calling. My phone buzzes, as if it, too, is disappointed in all the life choices of my mom's only daughter.

Here's a fun fact: my mother has an actual sixth sense for when I'm at my most vulnerable. Like, I could be butt naked, sandwiched between two dudes, and have cum in my ear, and she'll somehow figure out that is the absolute best time to call me.

And considering I now know Grandpa Miles was a pair of opera glasses, it makes sense that she can spot vulnerability from a nosebleed distance. I think it may actually be a legit superpower of hers.

I check the phone, and yep, it's her. Trying to FaceTime me.

I groan, roll away from Gage's chest, try to wipe the cum out of my ear, and flop flat on my back, phone in hand.

Marc asks, "Trouble?"

"Sorta," I say, "Mother."

Marc looks at Gage for clarification.

Gage says, "Apparently, the mother-daughter relationship is a fragile balance of guilt and love."

I cover myself with the comforter and answer the call without video. "Hi, Mom."

She's perched at her marble kitchen island, sipping a half-caff oat latte, looking like she just rolled out of some mid-day melodrama.

I ask, as chipper as a person who just came eight times can fake. "What's up?"

"Aliiiiice." Her southern twang stretched out to fill the space of my entire skull. "I've been trying to reach you all day. What on earth were you doing that was so important you couldn't answer your mother's calls?"

I close my eyes and will my resting heart rate below 130. "Sorry, Mom."

"Sorry, Mom?" she snaps. "I just get a 'Sorry, Mom?' Because I called at 11, and again at 1, and at 2:15, and—now."

"Also at 12:22!" I hear my father far away in the background.

"Yes, also at 12:22! Thank you, Abby-baby!"

I mouth "kill me" to the ceiling, but neither Gage nor Marc is looking. Gage is measuring Marc, and Marc is sprawled, arms behind his head, doing a flawless impression of a man who is not eavesdropping. But my mom's new FaceTime addiction ensures he can hear the whole conversation.

My mom sighs, as if every decision I make is designed to personally wound her. "Please at least text when I call, honey. I was over here worried sick you were dead in a ditch somewhere because you were ignoring my calls!"

"I wasn't ignoring you," I say. "Just busy."

A scornful inhale on her end. "Busy doing what?"

"Uh…"

She sighs again—a full-body, Oscar-worthy sigh. "Never mind. I'm sure the answer is 'Gage.' Honestly, honey, you're going to get a UTI. Anyway, I called to ask what you are wearing to your Aunt Janice's birthday dinner tonight."

"Mom. We talked about this. I'm not going to dinner tonight."

She snorts. "Nonsense. Gage's dick isn't going anywhere."

I glance at Gage, who's now measuring Marc's upper arm with his thumb and index finger. Marc flexes for him, which is both ridiculous and hot.

I do not want to go to my aunt's birthday dinner, because when you put my mom and aunt in the same room, it's a non-stop battle royale of sibling rivalry that I always end up getting caught in the middle of until they eventually settle on grilling me about getting a better job, a better apartment, a better man—which, now that I've made two they might actually drop that subject at least.

However, making a second one so close to the first is definitely gonna get some judgment.

I twist the comforter between my fingers. "Gage and I have plans tonight, Mom," I lie.

She tsks. "You know, Alice, she's your only aunt. It would mean the world to her if you just showed up. It's important to support family. Plus, she and Allen would love to meet Gage."

"Right, but—" I start, but she steamrolls right over me.

"I know you think these things don't matter, but someday, when I'm gone, you're going to wish you spent more time with your family. I know I wish I'd spent more time with my mother before we lost her."

I know this is a heavy cross my mother bears. She and Janice moved across the country decades ago, and she still beats herself up for it.

I wish I had spent more time with Memaw, too. She was a chain-smoking bisexual who wore muumuus and would scream "fuck off" from behind her screen door if you didn't come bearing gifts of pie and cigs—preferably both. *She was goals.*

And, honestly, my mom and aunt can be equally cool when they're not ganging up on me…

Fuck…she's gonna convince me, isn't she?

And I know Gage would be happy to see my dad and meet Uncle Allen.

My eyes flick to the men in my bed. Gage is still measuring Marc, but now he's using an actual tape measure, which he must have summoned from the ether.

Marc poses like a catalog model, flexing and smirking, the Alice tattoo on his pec vibrating with each pose.

I suppress a laugh.

I grit my teeth. "Where is it?"

She lifts from her marble perch. "It's at Nice Thai. Saint Paul. 7:30."

There's a flurry of motion next to me as Marc scrambles to my side.

He says, with a boyish innocence more characteristic of Gage, "Thai food? I want to try Thai food!"

I freeze.

Gage freezes.

The world, briefly, stops.

My mom goes absolutely still. She leans in, as if doing so will turn my camera on, letting her see me. Then, with the deadliest calm, she asks, "Alice, who was that?"

I consider hanging up and moving to a new city—one with great Thai food and fewer mothers.

I rub the bridge of my nose, and I say, "That was…Marc." I can't bring myself to say more, but the pause is enough.

"Oh," she says, in a tone that would chill steel. "So, what happened to Gage? Your father was growing quite fond of him—"

"That's not—it's not what you think—"

"I thought you and Gage were getting along well," she says, voice syrupy with concern.

"Mom…it's…Marc is…Gage and I are still together."

"Oooooooh. Oooooh. Okay. I see. And…what was he?" she emphasizes 'was' with a giggle.

"A marker…"

"Bring him too. See you at 7:30, darling. Toodles." She kisses the air and laughs, all haute, saying, "Abby-baby, you won't believe what your daughter—" before hanging up on me.

CHAPTER 10
ALICE

I check my reflection in the window. It is…suboptimal.

If you ever want to test the limits of your self-esteem, try attending a family event with two plus-ones who are both physically perfect and metaphysically unqualified for human society.

And if that isn't stressful enough, make sure you're still leaking sex golem fluids from the marathon fucking you've been doing with said perfect entities. And, to really salt the gaping self-esteem wound, make sure that family includes a pair of women with discernment that could cut through the most capable: a mother who acts like your life's mission is to power-game her perpetual disappointment in you, and an aunt who put the acid in acerbic.

I contemplate jumping out of the car at a stoplight, but that feels a little dramatic, even for me.

Marc leans in and whispers, "You look exquisite. I hope your family is prepared."

I grimace. "For what?"

Gage answers, "For the beauty and majesty of Alice," and Marc's smile widens.

"God, you two are gonna get me killed."

I'm sandwiched between Gage and Marc, who, thanks to not being raised in the patriarchy, aren't manspreading, but still take up most of the back seat.

Gage is holding my left hand and is using his free hand to take measurements of everything in the car—the headrest, the seatbelt, the diameter of a vent—and then whispering the results into Marc's ear over my head.

Marc nods each time with a solemn hum as if he gives a shit how wide the headrest is.

I fidget with the hem of my dress.

Marc covers my free, fidgety hand with his, and Gage says, "When I am anxious, I make lists." He says this as a fact, but I take it as a suggestion.

I run through the short, but comprehensive list of "Topics My Family Will Use to Emotionally Garrote Me Tonight":

1. Job
2. Apartment
3. My appearance
4. The time I crashed my mom's Lexus in high school and blamed it on a goose—and still do
5. The fact that I barely waited a month to create a new lover

I shake my head and say, "That doesn't make me feel any better."

The Uber slows to a stop.

"We're here," Gage says, as if the driver wouldn't have notified us, and climbs out with a bounce.

Marc follows, checking his hair in the reflection of the restaurant's window.

I linger in the back seat for an uncomfortable amount of time.

The driver locks eyes with me in the mirror, nods, and says, "Good luck," which feels a little pointed and is definitely not the last time I'll feel judged or inconvenient tonight.

"Thanks," I mumble, finally sliding out.

I stand, frozen on the sidewalk, assessing the motley crew that is my newly formed triad.

I look like a perverted fourth-grade teacher who drives a magic school bus by day and fucks two dudes at night: blue dress with cartoon cats, a cardigan, and sneakers.

Marc is in the same three-piece suit he was "born" in.

Gage is wearing a bright yellow "HUMAN" t-shirt I bought as a joke, but, as a literal creature, he probably thinks it is necessary to identify himself because he wears it most times we leave the house. He's also wearing gray sweatpants, which I meant to ask him to change, but got distracted by…well, the reason he should change them (and the reason I might be leaking sex golem fluid).

We're early, but I know for a fact my father got them here exactly 23 minutes early—he always does—some dorky dad-calculator-watch joke shit about 23 minutes being prime time to arrive.

So that means my mother and Aunt Janice are already in there pecking at appetizers, sipping snooty alcohol, and talking shit about everyone in the family, especially me.

I should have pre-gamed harder.

Gage is radiating a nervous energy that reflects my own. He's met my parents but is nervous to meet Janice and Allen, and still gets uncomfortable in public. He'll be fine, though. He's so heartbreakingly earnest, I already know everyone will love him. At worst, he will say something weird and my mother and aunt will try to dissect him, but my father will calmly take his side and then later try to teach him how to tie a tie or something as he gets to live out his (won't admit it but I bet he's got it) suppressed dreams of having a son.

Marc, on the other hand, looks like he could walk into a war council and immediately take over. Maybe throw his dick on the table and say, "Now this is what you call a dick," while composing a sonnet that somehow solves world peace.

I don't want to go in.

I want to run away and join the circus.

I want to crawl inside my own ass and die.

Marc spots my reluctance and pulls Gage and me into a bear hug that somehow conveys "suck it up, buttercup" and "we can leave if you want" simultaneously. He whispers, "It'll be alright. You're both perfect, even if they don't see it," kissing us on the cheeks.

"Ready?" Marc asks.

Resolve mustered by mustache tickles, Gage and I back up, nodding our assent and signifying our readiness.

Marc opens the door, and I lead the way.

The hostess spots me, then glances over my shoulder. She does a double-take at the men behind me. She sputters as if their hotness had evaporated her ability to speak for a moment, but composes herself quicker than most of the people who have found themselves in Gage's vicinity.

"Party of three?" she asks Marc, all customer service smile, but lip quivering.

Marc answers her, "Seven," and I'm not sure, but I think she has to brace herself on the podium to stop from melting into a puddle on the floor.

I add, "But they're probably already here."

She giggles nervously and says. "Oh, I bet I know the party." She leads us around a corner, clutching some menus to her chest as if they will stop her heart from exploding out of it. Then, with an awkward gesture, she points toward my correctly assumed family.

At first, I want to ask her how she knew they were my family, but then I look at the two radiant men beside me, and I get it.

My family is easy to spot—they always are. In a sea of people who look like they don't want to be noticed, they're a table of people who look like they want everyone to notice them. And everyone does. They're already mid-cocktail and radiating the kind of beauty that was literally bestowed upon them by gods and the compounding imaginations of generation upon generation of desperate, horny women.

Mom is at the head of the table, cocktail in her hand, and an expression that says it's not her first. She's dressed like she needs everyone to know she used to be—and still is—hot as fuck. Hair is perfect. Lips perfect. Posture perfect. Her aura is a perfect package wrapped with a bow and a little tag that reads, "I could kill you with kindness or just kill you." Her freshly lashed eyes are currently scanning the perimeter for threats (a.k.a. me).

My father is next to her, hand on her lower back, wearing a shirt with tiny calculators all over it. My mother bought it as a joke. It shows how alike she and I are—even though I don't want to admit that right now. Like my mother, his hair is perfect. Posture perfect. Perfect. Perfect. Perfect. But less annoyingly, because I'm a daddy's girl.

My aunt Janice sits across from them in a way that signals maximum disapproval and maximum boredom with minimal effort. She looks almost exactly like my mother, if my mother had less Botox, less joy, and black hair cut in a severe bob. She's holding a cocktail in her hand and her sharp tongue in her mouth, while her free hand traces the rim of her black turtleneck.

Beside her is a man who looks like he shouldn't even know her: my uncle Allen. He's huge, like, offensive-lineman huge, with a smile that could power the grid for a small city. Because he doesn't take up enough space by just existing, he's spread, arms wide like he's constantly prepared for someone to run into his arms for a hug. One of those arms is draped possessively across the back of Aunt Janice's chair like he needs the world to know he is the reason she's currently not lashing out at it.

And, now that I have the full scene in sight, I can tell that Mom and Janice are having one of their classic silent standoffs, fuming and waiting for the other to speak first. I can tell because my father and Allen are talking. They usually don't get airtime when Mom and Janice are going at it. That means, when I arrive, their full energy will be directed at me, instead of each other.

Fuck.

Marc takes my hand and leads us to the table. Gage follows as if we're pulling him behind us with a leash.

I feel like I'm being marched to my execution.

CHAPTER 11
ALICE

My mother stands up the moment she sees us and her smile is so wide it feels fake. "Alice! There you are! We were just talking about you!"

I have to physically restrain myself from rolling my eyes. "Hi, Mom."

I brace for a hug, but my mother doesn't hug me. She air-kisses me on both cheeks, then gives a little pat on my shoulder, as if testing to make sure I'm actually here.

Dad, on the other hand, is a hugger. He stands up, wraps me in a bear hug, and says, "There's my girl!" in a voice so loud it sets off a chain reaction of stares from every table in the place.

Then he pivots to Gage, shakes his hand in that arm-huggy way he does, and says, "Gage, good to see you again, son."

Gage beams, soaking up the attention, and reciting his practiced greeting, "It is good to see you again, as well, Abby, sir."

Gage turns to my mother and says it again with a slight adjustment for audience, "It is good to see you again, as well, Diana, ma'am."

"Gage, sweetheart, nice to see you, too," Mom says, beaming at him like she's about to adopt him, and pulling him into a genuine hug—which I definitely notice.

Then my parents turn to Marc, who stands patiently at my side.

"And you must be Marc?" Mom says, like she's pronouncing it for the first time.

Marc steps forward, takes her hand, and kisses it with just enough flourish to make my mom's eyes widen. "Yes. It's a pleasure, ma'am."

My mother titters, which I have never seen her do before, and sits down, still holding Marc's hand for an extra second before releasing it.

Dad shakes Marc's hand, saying, "Abby. Calculator watch. Accountant. Father," like he's introducing himself at a support group meeting for reformed objects.

Marc returns the shake in the style of a politician: firm, brief, and then a hand on the shoulder to establish dominance. He matches the greeting: "Marc. Marker. Writer-slash-artist. Paramour."

Uncle Allen stands up, eager to shake hands, as if it's some kind of game boys play with each other, and he's feeling left out. His mass shifts the table a couple of inches as he rises.

Allen catches Marc's hand first, shaking it so hard I hear Marc's bones crunch. He says, "Allen. Wrench. Contractor. Uncle."

When he turns to Gage, Gage's eyes lock onto Allen's arms. His entire body goes rigid with admiration, or lust, or fear. But when Allen shakes his hands, Gage says, "Gage. Ruler. Object of affection. Boyfriend," like it's a job interview.

The "object of affection" gets a laugh out of the table, and Gage laughs nervously, unsure if he should be joining in.

"I know who you are, from the group chat, buddy," Allen says with his usual chuckle. "You're bigger than I expected. You ever think about playing football?"

Gage shakes his head. "No, but I could try."

Allen laughs and claps him on the shoulder. "That's the spirit. Hey, next time, maybe wear jeans, yeah? You're making the rest of us look bad with that tool you're packing."

Gage looks down, then at me. "Should I have worn jeans?"

I laugh, "No. You're fine. Allen is just giving you a hard time."

Gage blinks, confused. "A hard time? He would prefer I were erect?"

"No," I laugh as Uncle Allen leans in to hug me.

He lifts me off the ground and says, "Nice to see ya, girly. Sorry, I broke your beau's brain." Now that we're up close, I realize he's even bigger than I remembered. He's a wall of muscle and tan, with a jaw that looks like it's never lost a fight. How I never questioned the otherworldly perfection of my family is beyond me.

Janice, who has been watching all of this with a smirk, remains seated. She states, in a low, drawling cadence that could be her reading your eulogy or ordering fries, "Allen, stop bullying the children and sit down." She looks at me and does what passes for a smile, saying, "Hey, kiddo." Then, she does a little salute wave at Gage and Marc, adding, "Janice. Human. Not getting up," before sipping her drink like she forgot we were here already.

And now that the niceties are out of the way, the test is about to begin.

CHAPTER 12
ALICE

The table wobbles like a drunk on a hoverboard as we all settle into place. *It's about as stable as my self-esteem.* Dad sits, not at my mother's side, but at the side opposite her. I'm once again between Marc and Gage, where I suspect I will find myself for the remainder of my life.

Before anyone can comment on my life's failures, Allen grips the table, shaking it violently, and nearly spilling everyone's drinks. "Lose bolt," he says.

Gage grabs the waters at my and his place settings with the reflexes of a man whose entire existence is contingent on being helpful.

"For God's sake, Allen," Janice says, lifting her cocktail from the table and sipping it as if catching it were her choice, not something she had to do to save it.

Allen winks at her, "Sorry, babe. You know I can't just let a bolt stay loose." He produces a wrench in his hand and drops to his knees before sliding under the table. On all fours, ass fully in the air, his upper-half disappears as he does whatever a guy like him does that produces all those banging and cranking noises.

Janice doesn't even blink. "This view right here is why I keep him around," she deadpans, giving him a quick slap on the ass. "Well, and he's...handy," she cuts a look at us so devious that it's impossible to miss the innuendo.

My mother—who gropes my father in public often—has the audacity to look scandalized. Janice gives my mother a sly look, as if daring her to say something about it.

My mother does say something about it. "Janice, please. There are children present," she says, side-eyeing me and clutching the pearls around her neck. I can't tell if she's looking at me for backup, because I am the "children" she is referencing, or because she thinks I'm going to do something equally sexually overt.

The banging and clanking stop, and Allen's head pops up on the other side of the table, grinning. He grips the table again and tries to wobble it, but now it's steadier than the building's foundation.

Allen dusts off his shorts, slides back into his seat, and wraps his arm around Janice's chair. He looks around the room. "Maybe I should get the other tables while I'm—"

"You've done enough, Ally-baby," Janice says, patting his knee. "Stay with me."

Allen kisses her temple, then says, "Always, babe. Let me know if you want me to fix anything else." He says 'fix' with this particular flair that makes me think they have some kind of pervy inside joke around it.

Janice smiles, an actual, unforced smile.

I'm so shocked that I nearly choke on my own tongue.

Even Mom seems surprised. Janice smiles about as often as Mount Rushmore.

Allen notices us gaping and laughs, "Lucky for me, she needed those curtains hung over thirty years ago, huh?"

Janice raises a single brow, wicked as ever. "Lucky for him, he was the first tool I found lying around."

Allen looks at her with absolute adoration. "Yeah, a screwdriver would have been a better man for that particular job, but I turned it around."

Janice leans over, runs her nails along his forearm, and purrs, "Good thing I don't know jack all about tools."

"Well, didn't know. Now you certainly know jack all about tools," he pulls her chair closer, and for a moment, I'm worried the two might start fucking right here in the restaurant.

The way my mom pivots the conversation so quickly, you'd think she was part wobbly table—*who knows, maybe she is.*

Mom turns from them, trying not to watch whatever is about to go down in their direction, and says, "So, Alice, when were you going to tell me you made a new boyfriend?" There is a glint in her eye that signals she's not even remotely pretending to be subtle about her line of questioning.

"Uh, well," I start, but the words dry up in my throat.

"Don't be shy, honey," Mom purrs, "I want to hear all about him." She perches her head on her hand and leans forward. It's meant to read as engaged, interested, but it's more like a predator waiting for the injured to break from the herd. "What led you to make another man so soon? Why a marker?"

Marc, sitting to my right, doesn't so much as flinch. He sips his water as if it were the finest scotch.

Gage flicks at his retractable measuring tape attached to his hip—a fitting fidget toy.

I do what I always do when my mother asks me a question: stall. "Well, you know, it's a long story."

There's a beat, and then Marc rescues me, resting his hand over mine on the table. "I was Gage's idea."

Every head at the table whips toward Gage, who freezes mid-water sip and nearly drowns himself before recovering. "That is accurate," Gage says. "I requested that he be given life before he dried out."

"Oh?" Mom asks, sipping her drink and raising her eyebrow.

Gage, unable to resist the prying of my mother and afflicted with the desire to please her, "Yes. I had fond memories of our time together in the junk drawer and thought he could assist me in taking care of her."

Janice's eyes glint as she joins her sister's hunt—two predators now circling their prey. She asks, "Taking care of her?"

Allen's grin widens. He's a happy-go-lucky guy, but he's also a shit-stirrer. I'm pretty sure this is probably the reason she keeps him around, not just his ass.

Allen laughs, "Well, the women in this family are insatiable. It's understandable that a shiny new bolt like you would need assistance. Although I'm surprised considering your hardware."

Kill me. Kill me now.

My dad, also a fidgeter, turns the dial on his watch as if it will time-travel him to a point when this conversation is over.

Gage, the sweet little clueless puppy that he is, "My hardware?"

My mom, drunker than I realized and used to communicating with an overly literal man, pats his hand, "He's teasing you, sweetheart. He's making a comment about your penis."

Gage blushes and straightens up. "My purpose is to measure up."

Marc, seeing an opportunity to save Gage from further social embarrassment. "Gage is more than adequate in that regard."

I place my face in my hands, "Normal families don't talk like this, y'all."

Janice, whose southern accent is usually repressed by monotone and her extended time in Minnesota, is apparently also drunker than I suspect, because it comes out when she says, "Oh, honey, we are not a normal family."

Dad, who has also adopted Gage as a surrogate son—he and Mom may actually like Gage more than they like me—grins at Gage, "So, son, how are you adjusting to this new configuration?"

Gage beams. "I'm very happy."

Allen smirks. "Marc caulks some of the holes in your relationship, huh?"

Gage looks at me, confused.

I groan, "Uncle Allen, please stop teasing Gage."

Dad puts his hand on Gage's shoulder, "He teased me like this, too, when I was new. It means he likes you—at least that's what Diana told me, and I choose to keep believing it."

Mom twirls her cocktail, as if it were a device used to turn the conversation to a subject of her liking. She leans in, and like her cocktail, her voice is syrupy sweet with a sharp underpinning when she says, "Just be careful, sweetheart. Don't go making more men than you can afford. Emotionally or, you know, financially." She tucks a loose red strand behind her ear.

Masterful conversational tactician she is, my mom can find the thread tying any subject to her favorite: criticizing my career.

CHAPTER 13
ALICE

Mom's eyes dart to Janice as she volleys the conversation to her repartee partner. It's so quick, it would be almost imperceptible if I weren't watching for it. Janice, who's got the same opera glasses half in her as my mother, doesn't miss it either.

And here comes the tag team.

Janice's eyes flick to me, peering at me over the rim of the menu she's pretending to review. "So, Alice, how's work? Still, uh…" Her gaze passes the conversation back to Mom, as if requesting the word.

And Mom supplies it, "Designing games," she says as if the concept is so distasteful, just speaking it makes her want to gag.

Marc and Gage place their hands on my thighs in a coordinated move of comfort, grounding me. Gage has seen this scene before. While Marc hasn't, it's comforting that he recognizes where things are headed for me.

"Yeah," I say, "I'm still designing games. We're about to launch the next installment in the series next month, so it's been a lot of work—"

Mom's face registers a perfect blend of concern and derision. "They work you too hard, honey. When you were little, I thought you'd be an astronaut or at least a math professor. You were so gifted. But you're letting this company work you to the bone to help design their vision to let people shoot each other in outer space—ironic."

Dad, always my cheerleader, says, "Her work is very sophisticated, Di. And it's a highly acclaimed game."

Allen, who, despite his ribbing, does also always try to smooth these things over for me, "I played the last one. It was a lot of fun. Building a game looks really complicated to me."

Mom doesn't even look at them; her eyes remain on me. "I just worry. You hardly call anymore, and when you do, it's usually to complain about money. And now you have two new mouths to feed."

Marc's hand slips from my thigh to the table, fingers lacing over mine, squeezing with a confidence that I'm now recognizing is his signature move. "Diana, you don't need to worry about Alice," he says, voice velvet and unhurried, soothing my nerves with relief.

He smiles at me, warm, comforting, reassuring, the way I assume a knight would smile before he slays the dragon who's been guarding my virgin loins. Then he adds, "I'll be taking care of her from now on."

The feminist in me floods my system with adrenaline. My heart now races for a completely new reason.

My mother, less taken aback but equally red-flagged, responds more quickly. Her eyes narrow and her lips curl into a smile that is all venom and pearls. "Oh, will you now?" She tilts her head, scrutinizing him with the gaze of a viper ready to strike. "And what, exactly, do you do, Marc?" she asks, clicking the 'c' at the end of his name and lacing it with venom.

Marc opens his mouth, but I cut him off, because he doesn't have an answer, and I'm not going to let this stand. "Actually, I can take care of myself just fine," I say, trying to keep my tone light, but Mom's eyes are already sparkling; she's scented the blood in the water.

Marc's smile doesn't falter, but I can feel the micro-tension ripple through his knuckles. "Of course, my love," he says, and his thumb strokes the back of my hand in what I know is supposed to be a reassuring gesture, but right now it feels repressive. "But now that I'm here, you don't have to anymore."

I turn to Marc, releasing his hand. "Marc, I do not need a man to take care of me. I am fully capable of doing things myself."

Gage leans around me and adds, extremely unhelpfully, "Yes. She only needs help keeping the apartment clean and with cooking."

I want to yell at Gage, but he's a) right and b) doesn't know the implications of the conversation.

My mom, a hardcore feminist but also a hardcore doubter of my abilities to take care of myself, says, "Honey, I know you can take care of yourself, that's the point I'm trying to make. I wish you would just apply yourself more. You have so much talent, and you are squandering it. You should be making more of yourself; instead, others are profiting from your hard work while you live in…I don't want to say squalor, but…squalor."

Dad speaks up. "Di, she is doing very well for herself. Please recall where you were in life at her age. I believe your perspective has been skewed by time and privilege."

Janice snorts into her drink, then shares a knowing look with Allen.

My mom cuts my Dad a look of utter betrayal. She clutches her chest as if she's going to lash out at him for daring to contradict her.

But she looks at my face, and the tears building in my eyes, and softens. She doesn't say sorry, that's not her vibe, but she does recognize she's crossed a line and tries to pull back. "I…I just want you to be happy, darling."

"I am," I say, looking down at the table, and at the moment I'm not sure if I mean it.

CHAPTER 14
MARC

I reach for Alice's hand, but it jerks away.

I want to apologize, but for what? I failed my first test, and I was so sure I had chosen the correct answer.

"I'll be taking care of her from now on."
"I can take care of myself..."
"...you don't have to anymore."
"I do not need a man to take care of me."

The slice of rejection was so clean and efficient, it cut right through to the core of me.

I reach for a script, but I was not created with one, only with a vague mission statement and the conviction that "taking care" is a virtue, not a vice.

I can sense everyone's emotions at the table. They flood me in waves, overwhelming me with the desire to fix them, cover them with a steady hand, then immortalize them in poetry.

Diana's eyes flick to Janice, who now fixes her sights on me. She peers over her menu, hiding her expression—though I doubt she's making one—and says, "Marc, what do you do, besides...Alice?"

I desperately want to please these women and correctly respond to their not-so-subtle probing. I can feel their deep love for Alice and their deep distrust of me. They would dry me out and cast me aside if it protected her.

Alice can't sense it, but I can. And right now, my answer is in danger of hurting her, so I must remain cool. I must remain collected. I must be a steady hand. My emotions are unimportant.

I lean back, summoning the suavity I was engineered for, saying, "I'm a writer. Poet, mostly." It's a true statement, with details left vague and open to interpretation.

Alice's mother—an apex predator in silk and pearls—nearly snorts. "A writer, huh? What do you write about?" Her mouth doesn't move when she smiles; only her eyes betray the intent.

The question is a weapon, and I know it.

The way to deflect these attacks is to show I can dismiss my own feelings with ease and remain as vague as possible. I leave out the poems focused on self-doubt and metaphysical existentialism and focus on the ones that prove I am devoted to her daughter. I answer, "Alice."

Diana leans forward, prepared to press me further, but the server saves me. She's young and pretty, but her recently brushed hair and newly applied lip gloss indicate that this table makes her feel insecure about her looks.

Allen is the first to turn to her. Her eyes widen, and, as if his smile is too bright to look at, she looks down, blushing, and squeaks, "Are we ready to order?"

Diana orders first. Then Abby. Then Janice. Then Allen. I take note of each order. I watch how they do it. Each does it slightly differently, but the general pattern is the same: open to the page, point to the item, request it, and smile.

Easy. I can do that.

It's my turn, so I copy their behavior. "I'll have the laab," I say, pointing at the dish on the menu. I do not know what laab is—I don't fucking know what anything is—only that I have written it many times and would like to try it. "And a Singha, please." I also do not know what this is, only that Allen spoke highly of it when ordering one, and I think ordering one myself will impress him somehow.

Alice and Gage order, and when the server leaves, I'm now back at the mercy of this family's judgment.

Alice's mother doesn't skip a beat. "So, Marc," she says, the last consonant of my name like she's a clock and it's ticking in her throat. "How will this poetry of yours be able to support Alice?"

"Mom, drop it," Alice says, tensing at my side.

I squeeze her leg and say, "Professor of Poetry."

Her mom looks pleased. "Oh, a professor. And where do you teach?"

I almost stammer, but instead I say, "I will teach at the finest school in the area."

Everyone's eyes narrow on me, and it's as if the atmospheric pressure drops.

I'm acutely aware that I've fucked up, but once again, I'm unsure what I've done wrong.

Janice, no longer masked by a menu, leans back, stroking her turtleneck. "Marc. How old are you?"

Before I can answer, Allen adds, "Like, physically. When did Alice make you?"

I joke. "Oh, well, I'm not a timepiece or measuring device, so I don't know the exact number, but earlier today."

Diana, Abby, Janice, and Allen gape aghast.

The rest of us gape confused.

The entire vibe of the table shifts from playful and aggressive to soothing and conciliatory.

Diana turns her attention to Alice. "Alice, darling, you just made him today?" she asks, the worry in her tone now softening from probing to cradling.

Abby leans in, "Marc, how are you doing? You okay?"

I smirk. "Of course," and hide my trembling hands under the table.

Allen shakes his head.

Janice says, "Ali, you didn't have to come to dinner tonight. I would have understood."

Alice snickers, "Mom insisted."

Diana retorts, "If I had known you just made Marc, I would not have been so insistent. See, honey, this is why you should call more—mix-ups like this could be easily avoided with communication."

Alice asks, "Mix-up? What are you talking about?"

Allen leans over and says in a voice that is suddenly confessional, "The first week is hard on us former objects. It's...better if we don't leave the house—the bedroom—the first few days."

Abby smiles kindly and says in a soothing tone, "You're doing great, Marc. Much better than I did in my first few hours."

I feel their kinship. I do not want it.

I want to be steady, permanent, indelible in Alice's life. Not another ex-object, just barely holding his new human shape.

Abby asks, "Seriously. You're looking a little wound up. Are you sure you're okay? You can tell us. No judgment." He cuts Diana a look as if to tell her, "Not even from you."

The truth is: I don't know how I am doing. I don't know how I feel. I don't know how to exist in this world. Only how to exist in relation to Alice. She is my center. She is my gravity. She is the source of all life. Other than pleasing her, I don't know what else I am to do.

"It's a lot to take in," I say, which is true and feels like a safe admission.

Diana chastises, "Alice, surely you remember what Gage was like in his first few days."

Alice's eyes widen in understanding as she looks at Gage. Alice sputters, "Oh, Marc, I'm sorry. Do you want to go home? You just seemed so stable. I...and you came with clothes. I didn't know."

Marc, the marker.
Marc, the man.
Marc, the dissapointer.
Marc, the failure.
Marc, the chauvinist, apparently.

The distress flooding Alice floods me. And I hate that I am the cause.

I'm overheating in this suit. A fire burns in my core, and the jacket holds it all in, but I can't take it off. Not in front of the table.

The tattoos…
the marks…
the admissions of need…
all hidden beneath layers of formality.

The drinks arrive, and the server places my beer in front of me. It's cold and sweating. I want to cradle it against my face.

When she leaves, the attention returns to me. Everyone is waiting for me to say something, so I say, "I appreciate the concern, but I am fine."

I've been pretending to drink all night, too afraid I would choke and cough out all my truths, but the heat is unbearable. I take my first ever sip of liquid, mimicking the way I've watched Allen do it, and hoping it will quell the fire inside me.

But it doesn't bring me comfort. The fire rages on.

Just as Allen had, I place the beer back on the table, with a flourish and a satisfied "Ahh," hoping the gesture proves that I am, in fact, okay.

No one seems convinced.

My collar is a noose around my neck.
I welcome it.
I wish it would tighten.
Take back this life I didn't ask for.

Alice reaches for my hand. "Are you sure you're okay?" Her voice is soft, and it wrecks me.

I want to shout, "I am fine. I am the man you asked for. I am the line that will never waver." But my hand betrays me: it's shaking.

I drink more. Large gulps.

"I'm fine," I say again.

Gage stares at my hand, the oscillation of it, then looks up at me with honest worry. "You don't have to be, you know. We're here for you."

I have failed.

I was supposed to be the caretaker. The anchor. The permanent one. But here I am, shivering in the middle of a family dinner, hoping no one notices the crack in the center of me.

I put on my smoothest voice. "Seriously, I am remarkable. You are worrying over nothing."

The suit is too hot.
The room is too loud.
The lights are too bright.
The smells are too sharp.
The faces are too focused.
The beer is too wet.
My ink is too dry.
My love is too little.
My mark on her heart is too faint.

"I just need to do that peeing thing," I rasp.

I stand, and the chair squeals against the floor—the sound shivers through me.

All eyes on me.

"I'll be right back," I say. "Feel free to start without me."

I try to walk with composure, but the air is molasses and my legs are new.

I make it to the bathroom.

I make it to a stall.

I cannot breathe.

I remove the jacket and hang it on the back of the door.

I still can't breathe. It's still too hot. I roll up my sleeves, revealing my marks. *Alice, all Alice. My everything. I am sorry I have failed.*

I sit on the weird open seat and retrieve two markers from within me.

Black and green.
Perfect and flawed.
Fake and real.
Fused. Confused.
Lost. Losing.

CHAPTER 15
GAGE

Marc left for the bathroom 23 minutes and 15 seconds ago and, using my bodily functions timing as a baseline, he should have returned by now.

Everyone is talking, but I am not listening. I am too busy thinking about the fact that there is an uncomfortableness at the table that I can't identify or solve. I am not equipped for family dynamics. I am equipped for two things:

1. Fucking
2. Measuring

And those are really just tangential skills. Skills I have extrapolated from my actual powers:

1. Having a 12-inch penis
2. Being able to summon measuring devices

Regardless of the angle I consider my powers, they are not helpful in this situation. If I were to remove my pants and thwap my cock onto the table, it would not fix the problem; it would only create new ones.

I want to measure the distance between Marc and me. Doing so has brought me immense comfort every time someone has made a joke I did not understand. But I cannot, since I do not know exactly where Marc is.

I lean back in my chair and look down the hallway Marc disappeared down. I can't see the bathroom. I can only see 7.3 feet down the hall before a wall obscures my vision. That means Marc is at least 17.8 feet away—the most distance there has been between us since his materialization.

I lean forward and try to enjoy my food. It is delicious, but the uneasiness in my gut makes it hard for me to stomach it.

Abby asks, "You okay, Gage?"

I want to say "yes," but I also want to say "no." It feels like a test. A social test I am, by default, designed to fail. *Is that another superpower? My inability to delineate between when I should be honest and when I should lie to meet social customs?*

But with Abby, another "numbers guy" as he calls himself, I feel safe answering with the truth—mostly. I aim for the halfway point between truth and social niceties: "I am okay, but I am worried about Marc. He has been in the bathroom for 24 minutes and 27 seconds."

There is a beat, and then Allen says, "We should go check in on him."

Abby taps his wrist, as if his brain requires tactile input to function, and says, "Yes. Let's all go."

I do not know how to process this, so I process it by standing up and asking, "Is it customary for men to go to the bathroom together? I have seen this with women, but not with men."

Allen stands up with me. "Sure is. Bathroom buddy system," he says. "It's a thing."

Abby stands, too, and sighs, "Stop fucking with him, Allen. He's still new."

Allen chuckles, "But his shirt says human, right there in bold letters."

Abby sighs. "It's not really a thing, Gage, but I think Marc probably needs us. Let's go, son."

Allen leads the way, and I trail behind, reluctant to increase the distance between Alice and me, but she waves me away, saying, "Go. Check on Marc."

Allen pushes the bathroom door open slowly as if he expects to find something catastrophic on the other side. "Marc, ya in here, buddy?" Allen asks, the normal happy cadence of his voice coated in concern.

There are two stalls. One is swung wide open, not containing Marc. The other is closed shut, obscuring Marc but for his perfectly polished shoes.

There is a sound I can't quite identify: a hurried scuffle, squeaking, scratching sound. "Marc?" I ask.

"I'm fine," Marc says, as if it's his motto. His voice is not fine, and I did not ask, all of which makes me think he is not fine.

Allen knocks on the door, gently for a man with hands the size of dinner plates—literally, I checked. "You sure, buddy? We're getting a bit worried about you. Taking your first dump?"

There is a long pause before Marc replies, "Define dump."

"I'll take that as a no," Allen chuckles. "How about you open the door up for us? I'd really prefer not to take it off its hinges." He scratches his temple with a screwdriver that he materialized, and I assume he is prepared to use it for just that job.

The door opens to reveal an explosion of green and black ink, marking every square inch of the stall walls.

Marc sits at the center of it. His jacket is off, sleeves rolled up, and the black inked tattoos of his arms have been filled with green ink. He's clutching two markers, one in each fist—green and black—and holding them as if they are the heaviest things in the world. He's not wearing his glasses; they're on the little metal shelf, with green dicks drawn on the lenses. His face is wet with tears, and his eyes are bright red. *He's been crying. Why is he crying?*

"Hey," Marc says, and it is the saddest "hey" I have ever heard.

Allen steps back and lets Abby push forward into the stall. He kneels in front of Marc and asks, "Hey, Marc? You okay? Did you hurt yourself?" checking his arms and body for wounds.

Marc shakes his head. "I'm fine," he says again, and now I know it is definitely a lie. This does not look fine.

I'm frozen, unsure what to do.

Marc is my friend. He needs me.

But what can a 12-inch dick and/or measuring stick do in this moment?

Abby unrolls some toilet paper and offers it to Marc. "Hey, hey, it's okay. This is normal, son. The first week is hell. This happens to all of us on our first day in our new casing."

Marc looks at the wad of paper in his hand.

Allen leans on the stall wall and pantomimes tapping his face. "Dab, don't wipe."

I want to say something comforting, but I do not know what to say. I blurt out, "My first day, I cried because I didn't understand how my erections worked or how to eat and sleep. Alice gave me cupcakes and a blowjob, and that really helped."

Allen laughs, and Abby winces.

Abby says, "Umm, Gage, could you maybe not talk about my daughter blowing you?"

I ask, "Oh…are…are blowjobs bad?"

Allen laughs, which he seems to always do, and says, "No, buddy. They're good. Real good. Guys just don't like to hear about their daughters doing them."

"Oh…should I also not mention—?"

Abby cuts me off. "Yes, do not finish that sentence. How would you like to hear about your daughter getting dicked down by that?" He nods toward my crotch.

"I do not have a daughter. But if I were to have one, I would obtain her by dicking down your daughter with this, correct?"

Allen claps me on the back, "God, I love this kid. He's just like you used to be, Abs." He wraps his large arms around my shoulder and musses my hair.

Allen leaves his arm around my shoulder, but my question still hasn't been answered. I'm afraid I will upset Abby, so I whisper to Allen, "I just want to make sure I understand: the implication is that blowjobs and cupcakes will not fix Marc, correct?"

Allen shrugs. "Dunno, buddy. But probably not. Don't worry, we'll figure it out."

CHAPTER 16
MARC

Abby dabs a crumpled bouquet of paper on my cheeks. "You want to tell us what's going on, son?"

Son. I'm not sure why, but the term of endearment feels like it's the steady hand around me I've been craving.

I inhale.

"I fucked up," I say. It comes out garbled, but the men nod as if they've heard this before from other new things-turned-men.

Abacus sits back, hands on his knees. "Did you kill anyone?"

"No."

"Did you hurt my daughter?"

"…No?"

"Then you didn't fuck up." He speaks in a way that is so no-nonsense, I almost believe what he says is true. "Tell me what's actually wrong."

I clutch the markers tighter. "It's just that…I can't be what Alice wants."

Abby asks, "Why can't you?"

"She made me to take care of her. To be a steady hand. But I'm…" I gesture at the walls. They're covered in layered over-writings of Alice's name; cartoon renderings of her; furious, desperate poems about longing; and an extremely accurate sketch of my own skull, split open and leaking green, because sometimes the best art doesn't require you to think too hard to interpret.

Abby gives a little smile. "First, I need you to know: my daughter doesn't even know what the fuck she wants. No woman in this family does."

Allen nearly shouts, "Preach." He chuckles a moment, then points at Gage. "You think she really wanted 12 inches? No woman really wants that much dick. But she kept him around anyway."

Gage brightens. "It is true. Alice did not know what she wanted when she made me. She just wanted a boyfriend with a big dick. Now she often says, 'Oh, God, Gage, that is too much, you are going to destroy me,' but she still likes me because I am, and I quote, 'a golden retriever who can make omelets.'"

Allen cackles.

Abby looks at Gage with both compassion and annoyance.

Gage chirps, "Sorry."

Abby continues. "Second, she made you, but you get to decide who you are going to be. This whole thing," he waves his hand in the air, "this life we were given. It's ours to decide. Not theirs."

Allen chimes in. "Look at me. You've met Janice. You think a huge linebacker who talks about power tools and football is what that angsty little beauty hoped to conjure up? Hell no. When Janice made me, she was hoping for a scrawny emo twink drenched in gunmetal black. I was so torqued up trying to be that for her, I couldn't even sleep. But I evolved. I adapted. I loosened up. The objects that do the best are the ones that keep evolving. That's what makes us human."

Abby grabs my shoulder. "The point is, you be you. The you that you want to be. And if you do that, I bet you'll find out that's the version of you she really wanted all along."

Allen says, "Damn, Abs, that's poetic."

Abby shrugs, "Yeah, well, I've been perfecting it for a long time."

I ask, "But…but what if I'm not the version of me she actually wants?"

Abby sighs. "Then, at least you'll be the version you want. This gift of theirs: it's as much a gift for us as it is for them. Don't let it be a curse by living a life you don't actually want."

I press my palms to my eyes. "But I don't even know who I am. I'm not even…one marker. I'm a fake. A composite."

Abby cocks his head. "You wanna rewind that for me?"

"I'm two markers. A green cap on a barrel with black ink. The other parts of me are still in the drawer or dried out, covered in dust under her fridge. Even when I was the two markers, she just wanted the serious version of me. She only ever used my green ink for dumb stuff. When she couldn't find the black cap…she just…put the green cap on the black marker, and just let the green part of me dry out. And she doesn't even remember doing it…" I hold up my hands, presenting the two markers as evidence of my deception. "Now, I'm two in one. Or one masquerading as the other. I don't even know."

Abby leans closer, voice softer. "I've never told a soul this, but…I was a display model. My band got damaged, and…well, it got swapped out before I even met Diana. I know how you feel, but don't look at this as a flaw. It makes…makes you a dynamic character."

Abby seems so put together. To hear he was, well, two parts put together, is surprising.

Abby continues, "The war inside you will die down all in due time. I promise. Just relax. Trust yourself. Trust Alice. Trust Gage. He'll help you. We all will."

I nod, not trusting my voice, let alone myself.

Gage beams at me. "Once you have a phone, I can add you to the group chat. It is called 'Things with Thoughts.' It is like a support group for all the former objects in the extended family."

Allen leans in. "There's more of us than you'd think. If you ever wanna talk about, you know, what it was like before, there are folks in the group who remember being everything from a press-on nail to a Ferrari."

I nod. I want to say thank you, but I'm not sure how to do it without sounding like I'm about to cry again.

I settle for a weak "I appreciate it."

Allen says, "You're one of us now. Welcome to the club."

Gage derails, "How was a Ferrari—"

Allen cuts him off and says, "Ask Rosa in the chat later. She loves to tell her origin story."

Gage nods, then steps forward, into the stall beside Abby. He wraps his arms around me, tight, and says, "You are not a fake, Marc. And you will always be my friend." In the enclosed space, the hug is awkward, but it's comforting all the same.

"Thank you," I manage.

Gage lets go and wipes his eyes, which are leaking the same lubricant mine have been. "It helps to say what you feel. You should tell Alice. She is not always good at noticing, but she will listen if you speak. It's called being 'vulnerable,' and she appreciates when I do it."

Abby nods. "He's right. She's all sarcasm and jokes, but she's actually incredibly kind. She has a big heart."

Allen jerks his head, as if there is a string attached between his head and my body and he's trying to yank me out of the stall with it. "Come on, buddy. Let's get you cleaned up and get you home."

I look at the state of me and this stall. The walls and my hands are covered in ink and lube. This must look like a lewd, cartoonish crime scene in which I've been caught green-and-black-handed.

The gravity of what I've done to the place sinks in. "The walls…I… I'm sorry…"

Allen cracks his knuckles. "Don't sweat it. I'll talk to the owner. This bathroom needs a remodel, anyway. I'll handle it."

Gage looks around. "You are correct. It is not ADA-compliant. This stall is labeled wheelchair-accessible. The door swings open, but it does not provide the 32-inch minimum clear opening; it should have been much easier for all of us to squeeze into it." Gage looks at Allen. "Well, Abby, Marc, and I, anyway."

Allen chuckles, "Gage, you found yourself a job yet?"

Gage shakes his head, "No. Well. Sorta. Alice says my job is that of a 'kept man' or 'trophy boyfriend,' but I prefer 'object of affection.' I would like a job with more measuring, though. I have two skills, and my current job only takes full advantage of one of them."

Allen chuckles. "Well, I could use a guy like you with my

contracting business. You ever get bored with whatever it is you do, call me."

Abby offers me his hand. "Come on, son, let's get you home for now."

I nod. "Okay. I really wanted to try Thai food, though."

Gage offers his hand, too. "Don't worry. We'll get takeout."

CHAPTER 17
MARC

The moment the Uber wheels away from the restaurant, Alice asks, "Will one of you please explain what the fuck happened in the bathroom? Why did my dad call us an Uber?"

Gage is on her other side, staring ahead at the little screen that shows the car's location on a map. He's probably comforted by the constant distance calculation.

"I'm sorry," I say. "I didn't mean to ruin dinner."

Alice scoffs. "You didn't ruin dinner. Gage ate his weight in pad see ew while you were in the bathroom. My mother was only moderately more insufferable than usual. Janice smiled. We're bringing enough food home to keep us fed for the next few days. It was actually quite a successful night."

She turns, pinning me with her gaze. "But what the hell happened? I don't get it."

I look at her, then at Gage, then at my hands. They're trembling, unsteady.

"I just…" I start, then trail off.

Gage reaches across her to nudge my knee. "You can say it."

I inhale. "I was trying to be what you wanted. I wanted to be perfect. But I'm not." I close my eyes and let the words tumble out, slow and ugly. "I'm not good at it. I'm not what you wanted. I thought I could be the caretaker, the steady one. But I'm not. I can't even get through dinner without wanting to crawl into a hole and die."

Alice chuckles. "To be fair, that's how I feel when I have dinners with my mom, usually too."

I almost laugh. "You made me to take care of you, and I can't even take care of myself. I'm supposed to be strong, and I'm just…this." I point at myself, but realize that doesn't actually explain anything.

I feel my throat tighten, and the next words come out raw and stuttering. "I'm not even sure I'm…me. I'm two markers mashed together, and I don't know how to be one thing, let alone one thing for someone else."

Alice's face scrunches as she tries to interpret the meaning of my words. "So you were having an existential crisis about…not being enough?"

I nod. "Yeah."

She takes that in. Then she says with a laugh, "Jesus. You really are my type."

Gage chimes in, "It is not your fault, Marc. It is normal for people to have feelings. Alice and I both have them constantly. I also was not aware of this on my first day, but Alice explained it."

Alice stares off wistfully, and I can almost see the hard shell of sarcasm peel away from her. "I get it. It's like you want to be the person everyone else wants, but you also want to be the person you are, and sometimes those people are not even remotely compatible."

"Exactly," I say.

Of course, she gets it.
My muse and my creator.
She is everything.

Alice sighs, loud and long. "Dude, you have no idea how much of my time is spent worrying I am not what people want."

I chuckle. "But you are perfect. How are you not what people want?"

Alice laughs. "Thanks, but you've got kind of a biased opinion of me. Anyway, I don't have, like, a philosophy degree or psychology degree or whatever...but...I think that uncertainty is what makes us human."

What is a human?
Composite of flesh and flaws.
Doubts sketched in their thoughts.

Gage says, "You do not have to be perfect for us. We just want you to be happy. And maybe make us happy, sometimes."

"That's the thing," I say. "I don't think I know how. Not outside of the bedroom, anyway."

"Okay," she says, turning to me. "If you're not perfect and you're not what I want, what are you?" Her expression is just like her father's. It says I don't have to pretend. I don't have to fake it.

"I think..." I say, "I think I'm mostly just a fuck-up who likes to draw dicks on things and write poems about longing, and who is sometimes capable of being a very competent sexual partner."

Alice laughs, genuinely, and the air in the car loosens by a full atmospheric pressure. "Sounds exactly like me."

I look at her, "Like you?"

Gage says, "Yes. Exactly like her."

Alice playfully slaps him, then grins at me. "So be that, Marc. Be a slutty poet artist with a green cap and tattoos all about me. I don't care. I like you."

Then she turns to me. "I know that I was kind of wishing for someone to take care of me when you were cooking in there." She points at her crotch, and my dick gets hard. Gage's does, too. Alice pretends not to notice, but in Gage's case, it's impossible not to. "But, the truth is, the only time I ever really want someone to take care of me, to tell me what to do, is when I'm getting railed. Otherwise, I like a man who knows when to let me drive."

Gage looks confused. "But you are not driving. We are in an Uber."

She sighs. "Metaphor, babe."

Gage mouths, "Oooh," nodding his head like he gets it.

She cocks an eyebrow at me. "Can you do that, Marc?"

For the first time since the restaurant, I smile. "Probably not," I say. "But I'll try."

Alice shrugs. "It's fine. We'll figure out what works for us."

Alice kisses me on the cheek, and the heaviness within me lightens.

Gage states, "I think you should tell Alice the thing you wanted most today. It is your birthday, after all."

I hesitate, but then I remember Abby's advice: I get to pick who I am.

I lean my head back on the headrest. "I wanted to try Thai food, and I wanted you to finally wrap your right hand around me."

She pulls back, looks at me as if I just confessed to a weird, but charming crime. "My right hand?"

I explain, "When you used to write with me, you always wrote with your left hand. I always wanted to feel your right hand, but you never used it. I wanted to know what it was like."

There is a beat of silence before Alice giggles and then dissolves into full-blown cackling.

She wipes her eyes and kisses me on the mouth, hard.

I can taste the lingering dinner on her. Saying it improves her taste would border on blasphemy—she is perfect, after all— but I roll my tongue in her mouth, relishing its presence.

Gage smirks as if he has an idea as delicious as his dinner, no doubt, was, and says, "The app says we have 16.03 miles remaining. We should arrive in approximately 21 minutes and 15 seconds."

Alice grins, wicked and sharp. "Is the driver watching?"

Gage says, "Nope. From the angle of the mirror, he should not be able to see anything below our chests."

CHAPTER 18
MARC

Suddenly, Alice has her hand in my lap, palming my cock through my pants with her right hand.

I gasp as a shockwave ripples through my whole body.

She unzips me, slides her hand into my underwear, and wraps her right hand around my dick.

It is, in every way, different from what I had imagined. For one, I never imagined having a dick in the first place. But her grip is firmer, and her movements are more assured. She strokes me slow, then fast, and runs her thumb over the head with each upward stroke.

Gage watches.

"Gage," I command, "Take out your cock."

He takes out his own cock, which is, as always, impressive.

Alice doesn't hesitate; she uses her left hand to stroke Gage. She pumps him, not slow at first, like with me. She's twisting her wrist at his head like she's milking it, matching the relentless rhythm she's applying to me.

Now that I know what crying is, I think I might do it again, but this time, not from sadness.

Write with your right hand.
Use me like the tool I am.
I was made for you.

"Gage," I say, "Let's take care of our girl together."

I slide my hand up her leg and under her dress.

Gage's hand moves in parallel, hiking her dress higher.

I brush my knuckles against her panties—they're already soaked through. Gage's hand is right there with mine, teasing at the seams.

She whimpers.

The car's shocks are shot, so every bump on the road launches Alice's pussy into our hands.

By the third bump, her panties are pushed to the side, and our fingers are between her folds.

Alice moans so loudly we all check to see if the driver is watching, but his eyes remain glued on the road.

I slip two fingers in, and she clamps down like a vice. "Jesus, you two," she breathes, "that feels so good."

I'm drunk on the feeling. It's not just her pussy gripping me—it's her, needing me, letting me in.

The center of her.
Reality's origin.
Not a curse; a gift.

"Harder," she says, and I oblige, curling my fingers in the way I somehow know she likes, while Gage rubs slow circles on her clit.

She writhes between us and drops her head onto my shoulder, grazing her teeth on my tweed. "I'm gonna—fuck—" she bites my neck, hard, and I nearly come from that alone.

The car hits a red light. Alice's body tenses, then melts. She exhales a long, trembling moan, and I feel her come around my fingers. Her hands pause their movement and squeeze harder, as if mirroring the walls of her amazing pussy.

She recovers, resumes her strokes, and says, "Okay, now it's your turn. Both of you."

She locks eyes with me and says, "You want to come for me, Marc?"

She squeezes and strokes faster. Her hand is a blur, and my orgasm builds within me.

I'm about to come, but I want to see her suck Gage's cock first. "I want you to suck Gage off while I watch."

She leans over and takes Gage in her mouth, while her hand is still pumping me. It is—I'm somehow at a loss for words—amazing is the best I can come up with, but it doesn't do the moment justice.

Gage's eyes roll back, and his hips jerk, but she doesn't let him buck her off. She stays locked on, sucking him like she's starving.

She moans around his dick, and he mirrors the moan. The sound does something dangerous to my system.

Gage comes in her mouth, and she swallows, looking up at him like he's the only person in the universe, even though her hand is still flying on my cock.

She wipes her lips, turns to me, and says, "Your turn, birthday boy."

When her mouth wraps around me, I try to play it cool, but the sensation is so intense I nearly black out.

Her tongue works in tight, perfect circles, and I realize she's writing her name on my dick: one place it is not already written, but definitely should be.

I can't hold back.

I come hard, but she doesn't flinch as my dick pulses and releases within her. She swallows every drop, then licks her lips and grins. "Delicious."

I let my dick stay flopped and spent for a moment, my strength gone.

Gage helps Alice with her dress. Then they help me put my dick in my pants and zip up.

Gage was on to something with that birthday blowjob thing.

I close my eyes and melt into the headrest, asking, "Hey, Gage. You think those cupcakes are still good?"

CHAPTER 19
GAGE

Alice's head is in my lap, and she is describing, at length, the concept of FOMO (Fear of Missing Out) to Marc and me. "It's not just that you want to do something," she says, waving her hand, "it's that you physically can't handle other people doing things without you. Instagram relies on this innate human emotion for its algorithmic effectiveness."

Marc is under her feet and looks less professorial than usual due to the cupcake frosting in his beard that Alice has forbidden me from mentioning. He says, "So, it's like...existential dread, but themed," before finishing his third cupcake, which I am proud to say, he enjoyed. He claims he likes them more than Thai food, but I am not sure I believe it.

"Yeah. But less fear of death and more fear that someone will go to a party without you," Alice says. She props herself up on her elbows and looks at me, head upside-down. "Hey, Gage. Can you get the rest of the cupcakes?"

I nod and lift her from my lap. She makes a small "oof," then grabs my thigh in a way that is both horny and supportive.

"You're the best," she says, with the biggest smile, before flopping lazily back.

I head straight for the tray of remaining cupcakes in the kitchen, but I'm stopped when I spot my and Marc's old junk drawer. My hand goes to it before my brain does.

I pull it open, peering inside it, trying to recall what it felt like to live here. The memory is still there, but it grows more distant with each day. *Will there be a day that I completely forget?* I rummage through the contents, trying to remain respectful of my former neighbors' resting place, until I find what I am looking for: the black marker cap.

My breath catches.

I pick it up and roll it between my fingers, and the action is oddly erotic. The plastic is smooth, unblemished except for the crack running up the side, and something about it reminds me so much of Marc's cock that I feel a blush burning my cheeks.

I slip the cap into my pocket.

The fridge is heavy, but I know the precise angle to rock it so it doesn't make a noise—I performed this exact action on my birthday, when I measured it.

I pull the fridge back just enough to see the space behind it. There's a pile of unswept dust, but I see the capless, dried-out green marker right away.

I reach for it, and the moment I touch the plastic, I feel something. I can't name it. Maybe it's sadness. Maybe it's nostalgia. I don't know.

I dust it off, then rinse it in the sink, arcing to see if Marc and Alice are watching—they aren't. I stroke it just enough to clean it, but not enough for it to start feeling suggestive or nonconsensual.

I remove the cap from my pocket and snap it onto the barrel. It fits with a satisfying click, despite the crack.

Pleased with myself, I put the marker in my pocket and return the fridge to its appropriate position.

I wash my hands, pick up the cupcakes, and return to the living room, happy that next to my dick in my pants, no one will notice the marker in my pocket. *Is this my third superpower? No, that's still just the first.*

Alice is now draped over Marc's lap and hand-feeding him a cupcake. She smears a little frosting on his face, and he pretends to be annoyed, but moans when she licks it off for him.

I set the cupcakes down, then stand in front of him, barely containing my excitement. "Marc, I have a birthday present for you."

Marc sits up, pulling Alice up with him. "A birthday present?"

I nod. "Yes."

He cocks an eyebrow, waiting for me to give it to him.

"Happy birthday, Marc," I say, removing the marker from my pocket and presenting it on the palm of my hand.

His fingers tremble when he takes it.

He uncaps it, sees the green, then clicks the cap back on. He does this five times in a row, as if there is some minimum number of times this ritual must be completed.

Alice watches, eyes wide, and puts a hand on his back when he completes the fifth round of uncapping/recapping.

He doesn't say anything. He just stares at it. After 37 seconds, he looks up at me, and there are tears in his eyes.

Oh, no. I fucked up.

I sputter. "I'm...I'm sorry, Marc. I thought you would like—"

"Thank you, Gage," he says, and now he's smiling so hard that the tips of his mustache are curling upward. "Thank you for everything you've done for me."

I shrug. "You helped me first. When you were a marker, you used to keep me company in the drawer."

He laughs, then shakes his head. "But you've given me...so much..."

He yanks my hand, pulling me toward him, then kisses me hard on the mouth. I'm not expecting it, but I like it. A lot.

When he lets go, he says, "You are a good friend, Gage." Then, "You are also a good boyfriend."

Alice whoops, "Hell yeah, he is."

My face heats. I'm not sure if it's embarrassment or pride, but I like the feeling.

Marc grins, then adds, "You're also...a good boy."

I nearly melt. I'm also not sure why I like to hear it so much, but I'm not sure how most of my feelings work, so I don't stress too much about figuring it out.

Marc leans back, running his thumb over the marker, turning it in his hand, then weaving it through his fingers with a level of control I don't think I'm capable of.

He looks at me and says, "You know what happens to good boys?"

I shake my head.

He leans close, and his voice is a low growl when he says, "Good boys get rewarded."

He turns to Alice, and asks with a voice like dark velvet, "Have you ever had two dicks in you, my love?"

She grins, eyes wide. "No."

Marc winks at me. "Want to try?"

She snorts, "I don't think you'll both fit."

Marc glances at me, then at her, then back at me. "In my experience, there aren't a lot of problems that can't be solved with lube."

He places the marker on the coffee table, and suddenly his hand is filled with that clear, greenish, glistening gel he's able to produce. "Take off your clothes, Gage."

I do as I'm told, because I usually do.

With him sitting and me standing, my cock is pointing right at his face. He kisses the crown and flicks it with his tongue before smearing the lube down my shaft, working me until I buck into his hand.

He removes his own cock with his free hand, then lubes his as well. "Alice, take off your clothes, my love." Alice peels her dress off, tossing it into one of the many piles of clothes around the house. She's not wearing any underwear, and I can see the desire glistening on her already. "Gage, you first, baby boy. Sit."

Like I said, I usually do what I'm told. I sit on the couch, and I'm shaking, not from fear, but from the anticipation of what's about to happen. This is also something I usually do.

"Sit on his cock, Alice," Marc says, "ass towards me."

She crawls onto my lap, straddling me. My dick slides inside her so easily that I gasp.

She moans, and her pussy squeezes me like it's trying to memorize my shape.

Marc strips off his suit, which takes longer than we do, since he has three layers to shed.

He stands behind Alice, pumping his cock, glistening it with lube, and licks his lips before he says, "I can't wait to feel that perfect dick and that perfect pussy at the same time."

Alice writhes on me, and I press my thumb on her clit so she can get the perfect friction. Marc pumps himself harder and says, "Yeah, just like that, Gage. Make our girl feel good for me."

While still pumping his cock, he reaches his free hand into the air, producing a green marker. He stops pumping and writes something on the back of his hand, then returns the marker to the void. I can't see what he wrote, my face is too full of Alice's tits, and the angle is wrong.

He holds his hand up, turning it so I can see what he's written in large green letters: GAGE.

I stare at it, and a tear clouds my eye when he says, "You're mine, too, Gage."

CHAPTER 20
ALICE

Marc brushes a strand of hair behind my ear, kisses it, then says, "I'm going to fuck you, too, now, my love."

The words vibrate straight through me, right down the axis of Gage's cock.

"Okay," I say, and it comes out hoarse. "I want you to."

Gage grips my hips, holding me steady despite the slight tremble in his arms—the same cute little tremble he always has when he's nervous-excited.

Marc kneels, lining up his cock with my pussy, which is already stretched to a dangerous diameter by Gage.

Marc, never a man to hesitate entering me, presses his head against me and pushes, slow and unyielding.

The first few millimeters burn, but then the lube does its magic, and I open, then open further, then open more, until I am certain that there is not a single cell in my body that is somehow filled with these men's cocks.

"Jesus," I groan.

Marc moans deep in his throat. "That's it, my darling. Take me. Take both of us."

Gage, who has been silent, lets out a tiny whimper of awe.

Marc presses in further, talking me through every second. "Just a little more. You're doing so well. Do you want me to stop?"

I shake my head, or at least I think I do. My whole body is so electrified I can't be sure if my muscles are obeying my brain anymore.

Marc says, "Almost there, my love. Just a little more."

He keeps pushing, and when his last inch slides in, and he's hitting the deepest spot he can reach, the sensation explodes, starting in my pussy and radiating out to my fingers, my ears, and my teeth.

Gage's cock pulses inside me. Marc's cock is pressed flush against it.

Then, the two of them move as one perfect, celestial gift of a dick that feels so otherworldly I'm already seeing stars.

Marc leans in close, pressing his lips to my ear. "You're magnificent, Alice. Sing for me, my muse."

That's the moment I come.

Actually, I scream. I scream so hard it hurts my own ears.

My pussy clamps down so tight that, for a second, I'm worried I might snap one or both of them off.

Gage whimpers again. His hands are digging into my hips, but he doesn't move. He just holds me through it, like I'm the only thing tethering him to reality.

Marc also holds perfectly still, letting me ride it out. But once I'm done, he pulls back a little and thrusts, slow and deep.

"We're not done, my love," he says. "Not even close."

Gage, always the eager assistant, moves with him, matching Marc's rhythm.

And it's beautiful.

It's teamwork. It's poetry.

It's a pair of dicks so perfectly coordinated it's like they were made for this exact task and…I don't even have to think too hard about how it's exactly what they were made for.

Marc kisses me, his tongue pushing into my mouth with the same hunger his cock pushes into my pussy.

Gage kisses my neck. It's a gentle juxtaposition against Marc's intensity.

I can feel every movement, every twitch, every sound vibrating between the three of us. Every sensation ricochets through my body like a bullet of pleasure.

I come a second time, this orgasm is so fast and so violent, I almost black out.

Marc doesn't stop, doesn't even slow down. He just keeps fucking me, pushing deeper, pulling back, then pushing in again, until I am a mess of drool, sweat, and tears. My whole body is vibrating.

"You're so beautiful when you come," Marc says, kissing the tears off my cheek. "Let me see you do it again."

He speeds up, fucking me hard now, using the leverage of Gage's cock to piston me between the two of them.

The pressure is unbelievable. I can feel every vein, every pulse, every drop of lube slicking the way.

The sounds are obscene—slapping, wet, raw.

Gage is moaning now, unable to keep his voice down. "Oh God, oh God, Alice, Marc."

Marc slams into me, bottoming out, and the sensation triggers a third orgasm, this one so intense that I lose all control of my body.

My legs kick, my arms go rigid, my vision goes black at the edges.

I convulse, coming so hard that for a second I forget my own name.

But I remember theirs. I remember every second of this, every inch, every word.

I remember the way Gage's hands shake when he's about to come and the way Marc bites down on his own lip to keep from shouting.

And then they both come inside me. First Gage fills me up so fast I can feel the pressure.

Marc follows with a shout that rivals mine earlier as his cock throbs and empties inside me.

I collapse, totally limp, my entire nervous system fried.

Marc pulls out first, then Gage, and the sudden absence of fullness is almost as overwhelming as the fullness itself.

Marc kneels over me, sweat beading on his brow, and kisses my forehead. "You're incredible."

Gage is panting, and his arms are around my waist, holding me like he never wants to let go.

I want to say something witty, or sarcastic, or even just coherent, but all I can manage is, "Holy shit."

Marc laughs, then stands, his cock already swelling again.

He produces more lube and slicks himself up, then says, "You have one more hole I must explore, darling."

I look at him, eyes wide, and feel a new pulse of anticipation.

"Ready?" he asks, voice low.

I nod. "Um. Okay."

Marc flips me over, so I'm on all fours, ass in the air.

He drips more lube onto me, massaging it in with gentle but insistent fingers.

He works me open with one finger, then two.

It doesn't hurt, not with the lube and not after what's just happened. If anything, it feels perfect, exactly right, like I was waiting for this my whole life, which feels like a weird life goal, but whatever.

He lines up, presses the head of his cock against my asshole, and pushes.

The pressure is intense, but the lube helps, and soon he's inside me, slow and steady. He doesn't stop until he's balls deep.

I rest my head in Gage's lap. He sits languidly, head held back, dick still limp, and pets my hair, soothing me through it.

"God, you're tight," Marc says, voice ragged.

He fucks me, slow at first, then harder—his signature move.

I brace myself on the couch, feeling every inch, every thrust, every ounce of energy he pours into me.

Gage moves around to my front. His cock is hard again. He presses it gently against my lips, and I take him in my mouth, sucking him like I'm dying of thirst and his cock is the only thing that can quench it.

Marc grabs my hips and fucks me harder, each thrust pushing me further onto Gage's cock.

The two of them work together, perfect harmony, fucking me from both ends until I am nothing but a vessel for their pleasure.

And I fucking love it.

I come again, screaming around Gage's cock as the orgasm rolls through me like a tidal wave.

Marc doesn't stop until he's coming again, too, filling my ass with his load.

When he finally pulls out, I collapse onto the couch, completely spent, body limp and used up.

They both gather me into their arms, kissing my cheeks, my lips, my forehead.

I'm sandwiched between them, held safe, cherished.

But...if I know anything about sex golems, it's that the night has just started.

CHAPTER 21
ALICE

We manage maybe three minutes of afterglow before Gage, sweet, tender, irrepressible Gage, is hard again, poking his cock at me like a puppy nosing for treats. He can't help it, and I can't say I blame him; this is a man whose entire existence is built around being horny and helpful.

So we do it again, and again, and again, until my thighs are shaking and my head is full of the staticky buzz that happens right before you faint—*or maybe die, I don't know.*

Marc is relentless, too, but in a different way—less "outlast the sun" and more "every minute must be lived with poetic intensity or not at all."

By the time we hit the third hour, I'm a quivering, cum-stuffed mess, and every muscle in my body is vibrating from overuse.

The sex goes on for so long that I start to think maybe time isn't linear. Maybe it's more of a Mobius strip, and I'm fated to ride this cosmic fuck loop for all eternity.

There's a moment—a very special, frozen moment—when I am sandwiched between Marc and Gage, and I realize this is exactly what I wanted but could never admit: the fullness, the intensity, and being the literal axis around which two perfect men revolve.

Time, as I said, isn't linear. It's a series of stacked orgasms, separated by only the briefest of pillow talk.

When we finally call it, when our bodies finally betray us and simply refuse to move, we find ourselves collapsed on the bed, a tangle of limbs.

I curl against Gage's chest with his arms around me like a weighted blanket.

Marc is behind me, spooning me, with his cock nestled between my ass cheeks.

For a second, I worry he's about to start up again, but he just kisses the back of my neck and sighs.

Gage traces circles on my hip with his fingertip. "That was amazing," he says, and I nod, too spent for words.

Marc's facial hair tickles my shoulder. "You are a masterpiece," he whispers, "a study in excess and surrender."

I close my eyes. I'm on the brink of sleep, floating in that perfect liminal space where nothing hurts and everything feels possible.

Just as I'm slipping away, Marc whispers, "My love, may I ask a favor?"

I don't open my eyes. I just coo, "What, Marcy?"

There is a pause, then the faintest click. I open my eyes to Marc's arm draped over me, his hand holding a marker: the one with the dried-green ink barrel and the black cap.

He holds it in front of me like it's an offering, and I'm the goddess he's offering it to.

I look at the marker.

I look at him.

Then I laugh—hard. It's the kind of laugh that shreds your abdominal muscles and leaves you gasping. I can't believe I even have the core strength left to do it.

Of course, this is what he wants.

I wipe the tears from my eyes and kiss him.

Marc nuzzles my neck with the marker still clutched in his fist.

* * *

Curious about how Diana really went from a Ken doll to a calculator watch? Read *Abby: A Sentient Calculator Watch Romance (The Touch of Sentience Book 3)*, coming July 2026.

Want to learn about Marc's other halves? Read *Drew: A Sentient Permanent Marker Romance (The Touch of Sentience Book 4)*, coming Fall 2026.

Don't worry. Rosa, the former Ferrari, has a book releasing eventually, too! 🥶 Sign up for my newsletter to receive updates on future installments of *The Touch of Sentience* series.

https://www.imogenknowed.com/newsletter

A NOTE FROM THE AUTHOR

Thank you so much for taking the time to read *Marc: A Sentient Permanent Marker Romance.*

I love writing sentient object stories. If it's not obvious from reading this, it makes me a little philosophical about the meaning of life and what makes us human. I've also always loved a 'fish out of water' story, and newly formed humans are perfect fish for those types of stories. And then there's the part of me that can't resist a good pun 😅

As a high-masking autistic person, I often feel like two people: the me everyone sees and the me I truly am. Gage and Marc gave me the opportunity to write in a manner that is more natural to me (a.k.a. Gage) while simultaneously freaking out about how it makes me feel not good enough (a.k.a. Marc). So, this story was a fun way for me to scribble my own personal existential (*metaphysical?*) crises all over a page productively.

Please leave a review on Amazon and Goodreads.

If you'd like to keep up with my work, follow me on social media and subscribe to my newsletter:

https://www.instagram.com/imogenknowed

https://www.imogenknowed.com/newsletter

A NOTE FROM THE AUTHOR

SPECIAL THANKS

I want to thank my husband for his unwavering support while I wrote this book. Without his support, I could not have hyper-focused on it, writing literally every moment of the day that I wasn't working or sleeping.

To my husband:

Thank you for enthusiastically discussing characters and plot with me. Thank you for being okay with the fact that my mind was lost to another world for a while. Thank you for always putting food in front of me when I get so lost in something and forget my own body has needs. Thank you for always being there to help me recover whenever my mind and body explode from the world being too loud, too distracting, and too scratchy. I love you.

ABOUT THE AUTHOR

Imogen Knowed is a queer, AuDHD girly who hyperfocuses on creating fake people in her head. Instead of letting them stay in there, she writes them down for others to meet. She spends her days programming video games and her nights reading and writing smut. When she's not writing smut or making video games, she's hanging out with her family and pets (aka her "pack").

You can follow her on social media:

https://www.instagram.com/imogenknowed

https://www.threads.com/@imogenknowed

www.ingramcontent.com/pod-product-compliance
Lightning Source LLC
LaVergne TN
LVHW011031110826
845149LV00015B/3378
9781972670033